# Flotsam

# FLOTSAM

## NANJIL NAADAN

Translated from the Tamil by
**Aswini Kumar**

ZERO DEGREE PUBLISHING

Flotsam © Nanjil Naadan
Translated from the Tamil, 'Midhavai': Aswini Kumar
Edited by Mayuravarshini M
First edition by Zero Degree Publishing: July 2023
ISBN: 978-93-95233-09-5
ZDP Title: 59



This novel is a work of fiction. And the research done to portray different periods is only for fictional depictions. Names, characters, businesses, places, events, locales, and incidents are the products of the author's pure imagination based on his research inferences. They are used in a fictitious manner purely for creativity. And any resemblance to any actual person/s, living or dead, or real event/s, or locales is entirely coincidental.

ZERO DEGREE PUBLISHING
No.55(7), R Block, 6th Avenue,
Anna Nagar,
Chennai - 600 040
Website: www.zerodegreepublishing.com
E Mail id: zerodegreepublishing@gmail.com
Phone : 89250 61999

Typeset: Vidhya Velayudham
Printed in India

# 1

Shanmugam's trust in his periappa was beginning to prove as misplaced as mistaking a bloated, flatulent belly for pregnancy. Two whole years of high expectations and bitter disappointment have passed. But somehow he still retained a sliver of hope as thin as a strand of coir from the frayed end of a rope. Every time the mailman Thangappan caught sight of him and paused in his stride, leafing through the clutch of letters in his hand, a ray of light would shine brightly inside the dark cavern of his heart. When it would ultimately turn out to be either the German News, for which he had paid a subscription of two rupees, or the Voice of Prophecy from Poona, the dungeon would once again plunge into darkness. He would feel as though the whole world had come to an end that day.

But that didn't stop him from squatting on the parapet wall of the bridge each day at around ten thirty every morning, awaiting Thangappan's arrival. When Thangappan turned the corner of Poovathan Temple Road in his khaki uniform, holding an unwieldy umbrella and the postal bag dangling from his shoulder, to Shanmugam, he appeared no less than a messenger from heaven. His pulse would race. He would get up from his place, wiping the sweat trickling down from under his arms with the towel slung around his shoulder. Even the cool river flowing copiously under the bridge and the ample shade of the laurel, banyan and tamarind trees lining both sides of its banks couldn't relieve him of his fluttering pulse and sweaty body.

After that, how to spend the rest of the day would be his chief dilemma.

There were only three avenues for passing one's time in that village during the day.

One was Thirugnanam's coffee stall that purveyed sukku kaapi. If you had ten paise to spare, you could get yourself a cup of sukku kaapi and a fritter, entitling you to linger for an hour or two. Since the place was not exactly teeming with customers, Thirugnanam did not mind regulars hanging around. Furthermore, he was an MGR fan. This provided plenty of fodder for discussion. Since both of them shared an interest in cinema and politics, Shanmugam was permitted to run up a debt of three to four rupees. This perk was however denied to fans of Sivaji Ganesan, for which several of them harboured strong feelings of antipathy. But there were no other joints serving tea or coffee and so they would grudgingly obtain their fix at Thirugnanam's stall and fling the coins at him, as though they were throwing a piece of bread to a dog. Some would not even step into the shop owing to ideological differences. They would sit some distance away and send for their drink.

Thirugnanam was perennially on a short fuse. He always had about a sour look on his face. His customers therefore judiciously avoided asking him for credit. An MGR movie would be screened once a month. On those days, he would pull down the shutters early in the afternoon. As he swaggered towards the bus stop, dressed in a yellow polyester shirt, a dhoti with the distinctive red and black borders representing the colours of his preferred political party, and a handkerchief tucked under his shirt collar, several pairs of eyes would look on enviously.

"Look at the motherfucker strutting his way to the movies… We should quietly set fire to his shop one of these days…" some of them would mutter maliciously.

Apart from Thirugnanam's tea-stall, Shanmugam's other port of call was the town's Tamil library. They would put out magazines such as Kumudam, Vikatan, Kadir and Rani only in the evenings between five and nine. During the mornings newspapers such as Dinamalar, Dina Thanthi, Dinamani, American Reporter, Vanchinadu, Kanyakumari, Soviet Land and so on were available. Since the day's newspapers would reach the library only around twelve thirty, there would hardly be any one around at ten thirty, eleven o' clock. Utterly crumpled Dina Thanthi, slightly creased and wrinkled Dinamalar, pristine and fresh Dinamani would be on display.

One could always reread the article by Kanakkan that had already been perused the previous day. Or else one could go through the serialised story, 'In the Quiet of the Dawn' in the Soviet Land. If nothing, one could always spread open the Dina Thanthi and stroke the breasts of the featured film actress while secretly experiencing a hard-on.

As soon as the newspapers arrived, some eight to ten people would descend upon the library. Some of them would look at the cartoons; a few would eagerly lap up details of the double murder at Manavalakurichi, while others would read up on the speech made by 'Kingmaker' Kamaraj at Nellai…

Only Madasami annan would pick up the Dinamani. And once he had latched on to it, no one could hope to even catch a glimpse of it till two thirty in the afternoon. Looking at him, with oil thickly plastered on his head, a bath towel wrapped around his waist with a snuff box tucked into its folds, one would think that he would drop the newspaper and head off home at any moment. On the contrary, he would relinquish his spot only after the smell of sambar simmering in his kitchen signalled that his lunch was ready. Shanmugam was well aware of this fact and would therefore try to grab the Dinamani before annan's arrival. When Madasami arrived and saw the newspaper in his hand, he would sit there glowering and muttering loud imprecations, stopping only when Shanmugam took pity on him and handed him the middle pages.

Madasami annan was one of the few well-informed persons in the village. He possessed some agricultural land which provided him with grain and a grove that produced coconuts. These, along with peptic ulcer, were his ancestral inheritance. He was a committed follower of the Self-Respect Movement and had studied up to Grade X. Throughout his life he had eaten healthy, exercised regularly and, even at age sixty, possessed the remnants of a finely sculpted physique. He also had a ringing baritone. He was an ardent Periyar devotee. Whenever he presided over Pongal celebrations in the town, the famous song by poet Bharathidasan, 'Sange Muzhangu'— 'Proclaim with pride that everlasting Tamil is our life and our prosperity...'—would be heard. Even today, every time Periyar addresses a meeting at Nagercoil, Madasami annan would proceed there, sporting the ubiquitous black shirt.

He had a very deep knowledge of Tamil literature and was the one who introduced Shanmugam to the aphorisms of the Tolkappiyam. Thanks to him, Shanmugam had proved very good with verbs and adjectives at school. And this association had guided him far beyond the mundane into the more esoteric realms of Tamil grammar. Madasami annan had also imbibed other great works of Tamil such as Nannul, Kaarigai and Alankaram. But unfortunately this great grammarian was weak in maths. Even as he topped the class in every other subject, maths proved to be his Waterloo. He had to give up his studies when he flunked maths in Grade X.

If Madasami annan had commandeered the Dinamani, Shanmugam's final resort would be the porch that ran around the Sathankoil temple. That place was a university of sorts.

A strategic board game of Lambs and Tigers would be in full flow on the south side of the verandah. The north side would see a few idlers snoring away even at that time of the morning. The verandah located in front of the temple's sanctum had balustrade walls enclosing an area shaded from the sun and rains. Someone would be reading a novel. Six others would be engrossed in a serious card game. Each player would have an advisor at his elbow offering helpful suggestions.

"Why not discard the lone nine?"

"How about playing a trump card?"

"Should we discard the clubs or employ the trump?"

Without a single worry in the world, two others would be seriously arguing about the relative merits and demerits of a medication for rheumatism, or whether a second side was absolutely necessary when there was fish curry already on the menu.

Playing the role of a co-ordinator between these three areas of the porch was Andi Patta.

He had only one thing in common with Madasami annan. He suffered from piles whereas the latter was afflicted with an ulcer. But, unlike Madasami, Andi Patta was a strong believer in god. He would get up early in the morning, bathe, smear his forehead and chest with sacred ash and emerge resplendent.

When in the right mood, he would also burst out singing enthusiastically.

His stentorian voice could be heard, either resonantly exhorting the lion-hearted youngsters of the town to rally around him, or plaintively singing a lament wondering pessimistically what karma had in store for him in his next birth.

But when the two bumped into each other, fur would start to fly and, despite the considerable age difference between them, their exchanges tended to transcend all boundaries of decent language.

"Motherfucker…may he rot in hell for advocating the breaking of our holy idols. It is obvious the bastard's ulcer is a curse from God for his heresy…"

"Hey…watch your mouth, you son of a bitch! Is this how one speaks to one's elders? What about you? Going around the village singing and acting like a bloody siddhar… do you know that siddhars are only good for rolling around in the gutter, drunk out of their minds on their arishtams?"

"I don't need a dumbfuck like you to tell me anything about yogis …"

"Oh, yeah! Do you know that yogis end up being covered by termite mounds when they die? You are certainly off to a good start growing one in your arsehole…"

"Motherfucker, may your tongue wither in your mouth…" And the war of words would continue in this vein.

Shanmugam had the choice of spending his time sitting, sleeping or gossiping at one of these three locations. Being at home was not an option. Apart from the heat and humidity outside, the atmosphere inside the house was unbearably torrid.

Appa wore a perpetual scowl. Amma kept carping ceaselessly. He couldn't even ask her for money to buy a bar of soap. That would be sufficient to set her off. "As though we are rolling in the stuff here. Why haven't you gotten yourself a job yet? How long are you planning to waste your time roaming around without bothering to earn a living?"

He would go for his meals only after everyone else had eaten.

If he went even a little earlier –"Here he is. Obviously in a hurry to get to work on time…"

If he went a little later – "As though we are here solely to wait on you hand and foot. Help yourself to whatever is left over…"

On certain days, he would be left with nothing but scraps. Some days, he might get food that no one else had bothered to eat. Buttermilk was a rarity. The coffee that was served to him in the morning was no better than ditchwater. He might get two or three limp, dog-eared dosas or a few sombre idlis made from batter scrapings. Oftentimes, there would be nothing to accompany these items, and he would himself have to improvise. He would then prepare a chutney by crushing a piece of tamarind together with a green chilli and a pod of garlic, moistening the mixture with a little oil and seasoning it with salt, and somehow force it down past his stinging mouth and tongue.

Things were a lot better once upon a time. Whatever the others might have lacked, he had everything he had asked for.

There used to be a whole boiled egg in his lunch box nestled inside the mixed rice.

Exam times saw milk every night. There was cash for the asking.

He never had to miss a favourite film.

Even if Appa was short, Amma always had some spare cash from her milk, buttermilk and butter sales.

But all that was history now.

Nowadays he finds himself short of change even for a Charminar cigarette and a cup of sukku kaapi. He did not know how long this desperate situation would continue.

The only belief he held on to was that his periappa would somehow arrange a job for him and that helped him survive each day. But, as the days themselves went by, even that hope was beginning to wane.

It was possible for a small family to somehow survive in Kurungulam village if they possessed a couple of acres of arable land and a small coconut grove. Shanmugam's appa had inherited two acres of land, owned two milch cows and, in addition, had fathered seven children with an age gap of two years between each. Managing this household was a herculean task.

To compound matters, the eldest son, having acquired his Bachelor of Arts degree, spent his time merely roaming around instead of securing gainful employment? The potholes that appa hoped to fill with Shanmugam's earnings were numerous. Just the thought of them created a huge pit in his father's gut. No wonder then that some of the sparks from that blazing fire tended to fall on Shanmugam's head.

There was, however, no sign of a light at the end of the tunnel or even sounds of birdsong heralding daybreak.

He attempted the Public Service Commission examinations thrice during his final school year.

Railway Service Commission exams twice.

And once for the position of Clerk/Cashier at the Electricity Board.

Two attempts at the selection tests for nationalised banks. Several other efforts through the Employment Exchange as a conductor in the State Transport Corporation, a clerical position in the Devaswom Board and so on...

What else was a B.A. graduate expected to do?

Appa kept instructing, "Go and get a bundle of grass for the cows," "Wash the cows and tie them up in the shed," "Go, check the south side canal for blockages."

Though he would grumble under his breath, he carried out every instruction.

Nowadays it was becoming increasingly difficult to prise any money to pay for his job applications. When appa had his meal, he would stand by the threshold holding onto the door frame, looking everywhere except at his father –

"I need forty rupees to apply to State Bank..."

"Why don't you ask for a round hundred while you're at it?"

"It's not as though I'm asking money for a movie. The Postal Order is thirty rupees. There's commission on top of that. Two or three certificates need to be typed and attested. The whole thing has to be sent by Registered Post."

"Don't you think you have sent out enough applications already? Obviously no one is waiting for your application to arrive, with a job offer at hand..."

Then, if he begged, threatened and cajoled amma for a while, he might end up with thirty-five rupees.

The Junior Engineer charged a fixed rate of five rupees to attest a certificate. It was the same story whether you went to the Government Hospital or to the Post Office.

If you approached the Village Officer for an Income Certificate or a Community Certificate, it was a different tale there –

"Where are you from thambi?"

"Kurungulam."

"What's your father's name?"

"Ramaswamy."

"Has he sent any sweeteners?"

"......................................................................................."

"Oh, all right then…go and get us two cups of tea and some snacks…I'll have the paperwork ready when you return…oh, by the way, on your way back get some betel leaves and Angu Vilas tobacco…"

However much he wished he could tell the Village Officer, "Listen you…you're a government servant and issuing certificates is part of what you're paid for," he had to bite his tongue. In spite of his B.A. degree, he needed two M.L.A.'s certificates with every application. His local M.L.A. however had his residence in Madras. He couldn't go all the way there to obtain this piece of paper, could he? If he approached the M.L.A. belonging to the neighbouring constituency, there were a thousand and one hurdles to cross…

In that respect Nagercoil enjoyed an advantage. Of the seven M.L.A.s belonging to that district, five were lawyers at the local court. At least two of them were always available – provided they were not away presiding over some opening ceremony or obsequies. Since this was a recurring nuisance for them, they had on hand a stock of hundreds of printed certificates, pre-signed. If you contacted their clerk, he would simply fill in the missing details such as the date, your father's name, your name, the name of the village and so on. If no one was around, he would also ask for two rupees for a cup of coffee. For two rupees you could easily obtain a certificate attesting that a person as yet unborn or even dead was very well known to the M.L..A., and the non-existent person possessed a sterling character. But, without this certificate, your job application was sure to be rejected.

But still, even after having gone through all this hassle, who was ready and forthcoming with an offer? At best, a postcard might turn up inviting appearance for a test. But then everybody who had paid the necessary fees would receive an identical invitation. The test would be scheduled at Palayamkottai. Was Palayamkottai in one's backyard? It was forty-five miles from there. The test involved six papers just like Grade XI exams and was spread over three days. You had to reach the place one day in advance. That meant four days' stay at a lodge, boarding expenses and travel costs – who'd pay for all these? And after having gone there, if you feel like taking a swim in the Thamirabarani River, fat lumps of turd would float past you brushing your shoulders as you dive in and come up.

How long can a householder with seven children to raise afford such expenses? To him, thirty rupees meant half a sack of cattle feed.

The so-called peoples' representatives have all been intent on accumulating personal wealth for a long time now.

The local M.L.A. was of no use. He wouldn't accept money; neither would he help. He was as good as reed. However he had no qualms about securing admission into medical college for his own sister-in-law's son or brother's daughter.

There was always the neighbouring constituency's M.L.A. But to approach him requires the intervention of a local party bigwig. And that person keeps on stalling, saying every time that annan had gone to Trichy or to Madras. The local bigwig needs to be somehow humoured so he can speak to the M.L.A.

But what will mere speaking get him?

Apparently he will try for the position of a Junior Assistant in return for three thousand rupees. Of course, there was no guarantee that the position would be his. The three thousand rupees would be non-refundable in any case. There was no way you could go to court to recover it. It was an open secret that the M.L.A. had two seats as his quota. But who knows how many three thousands he had managed to extract on the strength of these two seats? However, rumour had it that if you did not succeed in the first go, the job would almost certainly be allotted the next time around. The son of the landlord at Thovalai had secured a position on this basis. Paramasivam of South Street also owed his position at Cuddalore to the M.L.A.'s intervention. Not just that, Paramasivam has now received a marriage alliance with a girl who came with fifty sovereigns of gold jewellery, two acres of land and a house.

That was his appa's secret dream: if the fellow secured a decent job, he could milk the girl's parents dry. Should he gamble six thousand on a long shot? It was like using a sprat to catch a mackerel.

But there was still some confidence left in Periappa.

"We must write to him at least once in four days whether or not he replies. We shouldn't stop. He's a busy man and it is up to us to keep reminding him so he can do something for us…"

And so, Shanmugam had kept writing for the last two years.

# 2

In Shanmugam's eyes, Periappa was an icon. Not just to him, but to many in the village as well. But there were several who still remembered him from bygone days when he used to roam around the village with his runny nose, ratty hair and sores all over his hands and legs. They wouldn't place him if you referred to him by his screen name–N. K. Rajappa. However, they would recall him immediately if you mentioned his nickname, 'snot-nose'.

Even now when they saw him, dressed in a pristine white 120-count cotton dhoti paired with a full-sleeved beige-coloured silk shirt, a zari-bordered cloth thrown over his shoulder, rings decking both hands and holding an expensive packet of cigarettes, they would greet him with the words, "Hey, snot-nose! When did you arrive?"

Not all boys who run away from home at age thirteen make it big.

He must have been born under a favourable alignment of planets. No matter how often it was retold, his life story never failed to impress: ran away from home and, for a while, pottered around Madurai and Salem, joined Saradambal

Drama Company as an odd-job man, climbed up the ladder very soon to become the private assistant and personal bartender to Saradambal herself, got blotto one evening even before Saradambal had had her first drink, joined Bala Shanmuga Drama Troupe and toured Penang, Singapore, Jaffna, Colombo...

This was followed by an entry into the movies.

'Entry into the movies' did not mean he got to do lead roles. At best he was the bedridden father of the poverty-stricken heroine who coughed his way to an early grave, a nameless king in a far-away land or the aged, lecherous landlord who lusted after the virtuous heroine, a fairly namby-pamby villain. In all, he had worked in about seventy, eighty movies.

What stood to show for all this was a house in Madras, a son employed in a foreign consulate and a daughter who was studying medicine. And about ten acres of land back home. Even though he had only performed meagre roles in movies, his close association with an actor who had a very large fan following made him a fairly familiar face in a political party. He then went on to become the President of the Actors' Association for a short while, and then Secretary.

Then, just as he was cast in that actor's home production in Technicolor – in the role of a heroic advisor whose valorous words, before he is hanged, provide impetus to the hero to rebel against injustice – the actor's brother walked into that part leaving him high and dry. Despite the actor's best efforts to bring him around, he simply refused to be placated and so his acting career came to an end that very day. Since then, he had given up acting in movies for good.

That was when he took up an agency with the Life Insurance Corporation of India and very soon became the top producer in the entire province.

Even today, Periappa enjoyed some clout both in political and film circles. If he didn't, could he have wangled for a job in a foreign consulate and a seat in the medical college?

Appa nursed a fond hope that a few strings might be pulled in his son's favour as well. It has been two years since Shanmugam inclined his head for a sprinkle of such grace. His head still remained bowed.

Periappa's annual trips to the village with his family would be grand occasions. A beautiful Bhavani floor-spread would be laid out on the front porch. Gold Flake cigarettes and a matchbox would be placed within hand's reach. The smell of Gold Flake cigarettes was particularly sweet. As a youngster, Shanmugam would stand next to him just so he could inhale its aroma. Periappa would shoo him away saying, "Go, go and play with your friends." Now he realised that his uncle was more worried about being seen with a filthy boy, unwashed and uncombed, with a runny nose and a large tear on the back of his shorts, his ass hanging out.

Leaning on two thick bolsters, he would speak of many matters in a funny, deprecating manner. A small crowd would congregate just to hear him speak.

"Have you met Gemini Ganesan in-person?"

"Is it true that M.G.R. drinks thanga bhasmam every day for rejuvenation?"

"In the movie 'Justice for Womanhood', Lalitha holds your hand. What was it like shooting that scene? Weren't you the least bit shy?"

And similar questions came from all sides. He would answer each in great detail. The talkfest would sometimes go on till midnight or even longer, with not even a pause during dinner.

Only Periappa was served coffee with sugar. If milk and sugar ran out, he would drink black coffee sweetened with molasses.

Even as a young boy, Shanmugam had found himself drawn to Periappa's manner of speaking. Never during all his visits has Periappa ever brought him toys, dresses or sweets. Nor has he ever pressed even a small coin into Shanmugam's hands when he took leave. Yet, Shanmugam had looked forward to Periappa's arrival each time with great anticipation and enthusiasm as though it was the advent of a festival.

Periappa would wedge a lump of lime paste inside the cigarette foil and rub it to produce a grating sound–nerupiru nerupiru– which never failed to amuse the listeners. He would tear a cigarette packet in half, shape the pieces into circles and stomp on them hard enough to cause a loud 'pop'. He would extinguish a lit matchstick with his lips.

When Shanmugam was in Grade X and XI, if there was no one else around to talk to, Periappa would riddle him with questions about his studies. He would ask for his Tamil textbooks and proceed to sing the songs they carried. Shanmugam loved to hear him sing Thayumanavar and Ramalinga Adigal. This is how the two of them grew close to each other.

As years went by, and his appearance in movies dwindled to nothing, the crowds that used to gather around him also tapered off. He would take Shanmugam for long walks on those lonely evenings. Shanmugam had picked up many, many things from those educative walks in the twilight with his Periappa over the bridge, across the sandy banks of the river and through the village. He was then in his college years, studying economics and Indian history. The French Revolution, the two World Wars, Justice Party, the Periyar Movement, the rise of the Dravidian ethos…Some epic scenes from the Purananuru…The mystery behind ladies' monthly cycle…So many topics…Many interesting cinema facts…The wordsmithery of great political orators...Satyamurti,Jeeva, Arignar Anna. Time would just fly.

Whenever he visited, Shanmugam would go in search of items that Periappa particularly enjoyed with his meals—dried anchovy, fresh carp, crisp spinach, sweet pathaneer.

It had also become an unspoken understanding from a long while back that it was Periappa's moral duty to secure employment for Shanmugam. But his Periappa had been unable to find a suitable position even three years after his graduation. It sometimes seemed as though he didn't want to help. But if so, there must be a good reason for it.

It is a fact that Shanmugam and his periappa's son have had some issues. But that was way back in 1968 when Shanmugam was in Chennai for the very first time. He had just finished his B.A. final exams and had received a call to appear for a test for the post of an Income Tax Inspector.

The mere arrival of that postcard had sent his family circle into a tizzy as though the job was already in the bag. Shanmugam himself had been dazed by the thought that he was going to Madras. A job, love, all of life's luxuries...and so bubbled his dreams.

A big crowd had come to Nagercoil bus stand to see him off. The air was full of repeated admonition and advice to take care, not to get off anywhere midway, and so on. Everything was novel. The bus took him straight to Thirunelveli with no stops on the way. It was 12.30 when the bus arrived at the railway station. Even though the train to Chennai was only at 3.00, he rushed off the bus, collected his suitcase, ran into the station and hurried to reach the platform.

It was May, the peak of summer. Hunger and thirst assailed him. To catch the 10.30 bus from Nagercoil he had left home as early as 9.00 o' clock. A cloth bag contained his lunch for the afternoon and idlis for the night's meal. He sat down on a raised ledge that ran around a pillar and began eating his lunch. It was tamarind rice with a side of coconut chutney and citron pickle. Amma had packed enough food for two people. A young boy stood a little away, with one eye on his lunch and the other on the goings-on around him. A short distance away stood a dog with a fierce gleam in its eyes and its tongue lolling out. After having his fill, he handed the remainder of the food to the boy and went to have a drink of water from a nearby tap. All this while, he kept a wary eye on his suitcase to ensure it was safe.

The train arrived at the platform at 2.45 and there was a mad rush to get into the compartment. He did not understand the need for all that pushing and shoving. Shanmugam had managed to secure a seat in a two-tier compartment. His ticket contained his name and seat number. Each coach had a reservation chart affixed at the entrance with all the passengers' names and their seat numbers. He checked for his name and got into his compartment. Luckily, his seat was near a window. Next to him was a family of husband, wife and a seven-year old child. On the opposite berth were two Muslim gentlemen with beards, skull caps and lungis, and two middle-aged men dressed smartly in trousers and shirts, whose expressions seemed to indicate they were unused to travelling by third class.

The husband asked Shanmugam, "Thambi, why don't you move over to this side and let the lady have that seat?" Unwilling to give up his window seat, Shanmugam pretended not to hear him and stayed quiet.

As the train gathered speed, gusts of wind came through the window. The land all around appeared barren, made up of reddish clay. Even though dust and cinders from the train's coal-fired steam engine kept blowing into his eyes, it was still fun to watch the scenery rush by through the open window.

Towns with names familiar from his conversations with Periappa passed by: Thazhaiyuthu, Maniyachi, Saathur, Virudhunagar and, at nightfall, Madurai. Thiruparankundram, the temple towers on the Masi Streets, the Vaigai river...

The condition of the Vaigai was a rude shock. The river appeared like an old and wizened whore. Legs cracked and swollen, a bloated face with dried and distended lips, sunken and crusted eyes, lesions on the skin, pendulous, withered breasts– it was bitterly startling to see her look like an old, spent prostitute whose time had passed. Thorn bushes along the banks, filthy sewers draining into it, a long line of people squatting and defecating on its sides, stagnant pools of dirty water. Shanmugam wished he had not witnessed this horrendous sight. In his mind's eye, he had envisioned an image of the Vaigai as it appeared in the epic Silappatikaram and in certain historical novels.

The train was scheduled to reach Trichy at midnight. He wished he could have a glimpse of the legendary Cauvery River as well during the course of the journey. But, at the same time, his mind still reeled from the shocking state of the Vaigai.

In any case, he would have to go to sleep in his seat. The man next to him went up to the top berth leaving his wife behind. The two smartly dressed men opposite apparently had reserved berths. The two Muslim men hunkered down to sleep in the top and tail position. The woman put her daughter to sleep in the berth, spread out a blanket on the floor of the compartment in the space between the two berths and lied down.

As she slept, her legs stretched in Shanmugam's direction and brushed against his feet. She was lying on her side, facing her daughter, with the left hand supporting her head. Shanmugam quickly withdrew his legs, and began covertly checking the woman out.

She appeared shadowy in the dim blue glow of the nightlight. She was perhaps around 26 or 27 years old. A body plumped up by childbirth. Both sides of her nose were pierced and bore 7-stone nose pins. In the course of her sleep, her sari parted slightly and revealed tantalising curves. Her thali was visible around her neck. Her sari rucked up to reveal her calves.

A female form lying nearby, his eyes roved over her body lasciviously like a hungry dog lapping up every last crumb from its bowl. He sat up straight in his seat and stretched. He let out two or three yawns. He felt the heat of his body spreading to his lips, throat, nostrils and ear lobes. He extended his folded legs and, as though by accident, touched the woman's knee with his toe.

There was total stillness within the compartment. Everyone was fast asleep. He began slowly stroking her kneecap with his toe. He wondered if he dared to use his toes to gently pull up her sari a little higher. Fear however gnawed at him. The woman turned over in her sleep. Her calves appeared as smooth and soft as banana stems. Its silkiness was evident even to his rough and calloused toe. His fever rose. The game however soon lost its allure. He craved for something more. But fear constricted his throat.

Shanmugam got up from his seat quickly. He securely re-tied his dhoti and made his way up the aisle. He glanced around the compartment for a moment and walked swiftly towards the toilet.

His heartbeat resumed its normal rhythm shortly. He leant back against the door with his eyes shut for a while, and then exited the bathroom. He went back to his seat and closed his eyes. The wind caressed his hair. When he awakened, the train had reached Maduranthakam. His eyes felt itchy. There was a big rush of passengers near the wash area with everyone holding their toothbrush, toothpaste, tongue cleaner, soap and towel.

As they neared Chennai, his heartbeat sped up. Houses dotted the distant horizon; there were a few factories. Tambaram, Mambalam, Egmore…

Periappa and Periamma had both come to the station to receive him. To Shanmugam, this felt like an honour equivalent to a 21-gun salute.

The people around him somehow seemed different. Everyone had a shirt on. All of them seemed to have sandals or slippers on their feet. Most sported clipped moustaches and trimmed hair. He felt like he had wound up in a foreign country. The language they spoke reminded him of pebbles rattling in a tin can. There was a vegetable vendor with a wide mouth, a yellow sheen of turmeric paste on her dark features, a huge vermillion dot in the middle of her forehead and an oversized hair bun with flowers decorating it.

Bananas hung in bunches on ropes rather than as whole sheaves.

Bus conductors made a 'phweep' sound with their lips instead of using their whistles. Curses being exchanged made no sense– kasmalam, bejaru, bemani – the language was totally alien.

Everyone seemed to be on their way to the 'market', to eat something called 'tiffin', or have their 'nasta'. Abuses were being exchanged in high-pitched tones. But no one seemed overly bothered by their virulence. A twenty-year old spoke to a sixty-year old with scant respect, employing the discourteous singular form of address.

Cinema posters were humongous in size. But, close up, the features of the actors appeared lopsided, like viewing a movie from the corner-most seat of the very first row in a movie hall. Mouths agape like an animal's, the heroes posed holding daggers or pistols in their hands. The heroines lay supine, with chests that seemed oversized in comparison to their general physique. Or else, they clung to the hero, all the while ensuring that their breasts were pressed tightly into his chest or back.

While he was used to seeing buses in his village displaying boards with only their destinations, here they were numbered 11A, 24C, 45B and so on. Garbage bins next to the bus stop overflowed and the stench reeked to the skies. Plump, sacred cows lounged imperiously nearby with nary a care.

The temples also appeared different. And they were dedicated to deities unheard of– Angalamman, Mariamman, Mahamayee…

Muniyandi Vilas 'hotels' were dime a dozen. Biryani was ready all the time. He vowed to taste their Chicken Biryani once he secured a job and received his first salary.

It had been four days since his arrival in Chennai. Still he remained totally clueless. It seemed to him that the directions themselves had shifted positions: catch a bus in front of the Gaudiya Mutt, get off at the last stop in Triplicane for a short walk to the University of Madras's Centenary Auditorium where the tests were being held. It seemed to him like he was retaking his B.A. final examinations.

His B.A. results were announced on the day he wrote his last test. Lists of successful candidates were stuck on blackboards and displayed all around the building. It took him a long while to locate the results for B.A. Economics. Kumaravelu, who pursued Maths at his college, said he had passed with a first class. Shanmugam's heart fluttered like a bird's wings mired in water. Together they located the results for B.A. Economics. After quickly skimming through the names of those who had passed in first class, he located his own name and Roll Number – 'R. Shanmugam – 4756' – in the list of candidates who had passed in the second division.

He was ecstatic. Particularly at the thought of the additional boost his prestige would now receive at his Periappa's house in Chennai.

Kumaravelu said he needed to send a telegram to his family announcing his result. Shanmugam too followed suit, happily contemplating the shock and delight that the news would generate back home. Kumaravelu suggested they go to a restaurant and celebrate by having some sweets.

Back home in Kurungulam, 'sweet' to Shanmugam, son of Ramaswamy, meant appam and candied cashew nuts that his Amma prepared on Deepavali days; the powdered rice and jaggery mix served as an offering at the goddess' temple on full moon days; the mini appams that featured on the menu occasionally at Thirugnanam's tea-stall; the so-called 'halwa' which was nothing more than pieces of coloured gelatine sweetened with saccharine on sale during the ceremonial procession of Lord Sastha on his swivel horse. It was only once a year on School or College Annual Days that he actually set eyes on 'real' sweets, such as Laddu or Mysorepak. Only once had he ever tasted a boli. That was when a neighbour of his had received a large supply of the sweet and had not bothered to open the packet for several days causing the entire lot to become mildewed. He had then generously distributed the sweet to every house in the locality and Shanmugam had received his share.

During his college days, even though his mind hankered to taste some exotic sweet or the other in a restaurant, practical considerations would ultimately compel him to settle for two dosas instead. Or, on days when he felt particularly adventurous, he would order pooris with potato curry or chapatti and korma. Otherwise, sweets such as jangiri, basundi, badam kheer, gulab jamun, rasgulla and so on were only names he had read in stories and serials in magazines such as Kumudam and Ananda Vikatan.

He decided that he would eat a sweet he had never tasted before that day. Kumaravelu would know all about that. A person who came to college by scooter every day would certainly be knowledgeable about such matters, wouldn't he?

The restaurant appeared imposing. The waiters were all in uniforms. They even had caps on. They appeared neat and tidy. They didn't bring glasses of water with a film of oil floating on top, with their thumbs dunked into them. They didn't repeat your order, shouting it out to the kitchen staff from close to your ears, as though deriding your choice of dishes.

Ice-cold water came in clear, plain glasses. It was distinctly pleasurable sitting on high-backed cushioned chairs, sipping cold water. The waiter came and stood by Kumaravelu, awaiting his order. Perhaps he was able to distinguish who was who between the two of them. Maybe Shanmugam's dress, hairstyle and appearance automatically precluded him from ordering in a restaurant such as this.

As Shanmugam looked on, Kumaravelu ordered, "Two Mysorepaks."

They arrived in porcelain plates sporting an unburnt brick-red colour. Two stainless steel spoons accompanied them. Kumaravelu very dexterously wielded his spoon to cut a piece of the mysorepak and put it in his mouth. For a moment Shanmugam contemplated simply picking up the sweet by hand and eating it. Then, deciding it would appear indecorous in a posh setting such as this, he picked up his spoon, placed it on the back of the mysorepak and pressed hard. His spoon made a loud 'clang' as it hit the plate and the bisected pieces of the sweet flew off in two different directions.

He felt mortified.

Luckily, the restaurant was not very crowded. Kumaravelu glanced at him askance. Perhaps even abused him mentally, invoking his caste affiliation. This would also make for a good story to relate to all their acquaintances as soon as he reached home. The understanding waiter, ignoring Shanmugam's guilty look, brought him another piece of mysorepak with a slight smile. Since Kumaravelu settled the bill, Shanmugam did not know how much the mysorepaks cost.

After seeing Kumaravelu off, Shanmugam felt a little better. The Mail contained details of the B.A. results. He bought a copy of the newspaper to display the result at home and once again rechecked his name and number. He felt that Periappa's family members would expect sweets from him. So he bought a tin of cheap chocolates and waited for Bus No. 13 to arrive.

Even though he must have appeared uncouth, dressed outlandishly in an ill-fitting trouser and shirt, sporting a hairdo that Chennai city had probably never seen before, the fact that he was now a B.A. graduate gave him a modicum of pride. Consciously ignoring the girls in the bus, he concentrated on the newspaper in his hand.

Last year, when his cousin had visited Kurungulam, he recalled how he was given The Hindu and asked to read out a paragraph from the newspaper. He didn't realise then that it was meant to be a demeaning test. He read out the selected passage with great affectation, putting on the accent of his English professor. His cousin was suitably silenced. Perhaps he had assumed a B.A. from Kurungulam was of a lesser calibre than a tenth grade student from Madras. His conversations with his cousin thereafter were heavily laced with English words.

The habit continued during this visit also. Shanmugam had learnt a few special words just for this trip – words such as 'synchronise', 'idiosyncrasy', 'enthusiasm' from his English guidebook and expressions like 'a hard nut to crack' and 'keep your fingers crossed'.

His cousin however seemed to overstep all limits.

"Shanmugam, get me a packet of Wills cigarettes from the corner-store."

There was nothing wrong about fetching a packet of cigarettes for him. After all he was his cousin. But Shanmugam felt a little put out that he should order him around this way as he put on his shoes to leave for his office, and with his wife hovering nearby. He might as well have bought it himself on his way out. Perhaps this was his way of demonstrating to his wife his superiority by ordering a B.A. graduate around. Shanmugam felt this was a contest he could not hope to win.

Whatever it was, there seemed to be some friction within the family.

The first clue had emerged from the conversation between Periamma and Periappa on the day they were returning home in the taxi. The rest came from the manner in which the daughter-in-law spoke to his Periamma, from the exaggerated theatrical poses that Periappa struck behind his daughter-in-law's back and from his cousin's permanent sullen demeanour and unwillingness to communicate freely with anyone.

His cousin and wife had their own room upstairs. Both were employed. Once they were gone, Periappa and Periamma would analyse the day's events in great detail. They had gone to see a late movie last night and let the food cooked at home go waste. Last week, when she had gone upstairs to clean, Periamma had found a halwa wrapper in their room. From the change obtained for a hundred rupees, twenty rupees had gone missing…

All this was not unusual in many households. Two days ago, however, when he was summoned upstairs and asked, "What do they talk about me in my absence?" Shanmugam felt faintly repulsed.

Unconsciously, Shanmugam had veered towards his Periappa's side. He had already developed a special respect for him in view of their earlier interactions at the village. That feeling had only been strengthened further since his arrival here. He specially appreciated being treated like a friend by his Periappa.

Periappa did not have fixed working hours. Since his dealings – canvassing for policies, collecting premiums, issuing receipts – were mainly with actors, film producers and technicians, he'd leave home only after 11 o' clock. Since he was in town, on Saturdays and Sundays, he'd take Shanmugam also along with him wherever he went.

He immediately recognised senior actors such as Sahasranamam, M.N. Rajam and T.S. Balaiah. He would stare at them with his mouth agape as Periappa chatted with them.

They went to a film studio – it was either Vijaya or Vauhini.

"Hello, anne! It's been a long time."

"What scene are they shooting? A royal court?"

"Anne, those days are long gone! You've to move with the times."

"Is the boss around?"

"He's shooting at Gemini studio today."

To those who enquired, Periappa introduced him as his younger brother's son, a B.A. graduate who had come to Madras to appear for the Income Tax Inspector's test. Shanmugam found this intro very enjoyable, particularly when some of them pretended to be frightened at the mention of the words, 'Income Tax'.

Even though his test was on the next day, after dinner, when everyone else had gone to sleep, Periappa sat with him on the porch and went on chatting for a very long time: the shortcomings in the field of cinema, the ballad Kalingattuparani celebrating the victory of the Cholas over the Kalinga army…

Shanmugam then asked casually,

"Periappa, were you ever in love in your younger days?"

After a brief pause, he replied – "Yes. There was a girl in our town, Krishnankoil, who used to live in the house opposite ours…she was dark-complexioned but very pretty. Smart as a whip too. But she got married to someone else and moved away. That's when I met your Periamma and fell for her."

"Haven't you two got anything better to discuss?" Periamma's voice was suddenly heard. No one knew how long she had been there listening.

Shanmugam got down at the Royapettah Police Station bus stop and walked towards Periappa's house. The sun had gone down and a yellow tinge suffused the locality as a prelude to the coming darkness. Anna and his wife were standing on the terrace.

When he saw him, anna gave a smile. It had overtones of mockery and ridicule.

"Hi Shanmugam! You're late today."

"Yes…the results have come out."

"Was your number there?"

"Second class."

"Oh, congratulations. Is that The Mail? Bring it upstairs."

Everyone was home— Periappa, Periamma and his two cousins who were already back home from college. He announced his news to Periappa. Everyone was delighted. "You're the first graduate in our family," said Periappa. He distributed the chocolates he had brought with him. As he was sipping the coffee that Periamma had served him, his sister-in-law came downstairs for something.

His Periappa related an interesting anecdote.

"It's not as though you can sell a policy across the table at the very first meeting. You need to tailor your approach to the prospect and wear down his resistance. For almost three years, I was chasing after this senior Chettiar, who had been talking of a policy for a hundred thousand rupees. But he kept evading me. I did not give up. I even made up songs on the spot to entertain him. He seemed to be enjoying all this attention but would still not sign on the dotted line. Ultimately, even though I was disappointed in the end, it proved profitable for the Insurance Company, for Chettiar dropped dead within three months of our last meeting."

As his sister-in-law was going back upstairs, Shanmugam handed her The Mail and some chocolates and requested her to give them to anna. While he was laughing at Periappa's story, the newspaper landed with a loud 'pat' on the floor next to him. When he looked up, his cousin was standing on the staircase. The chocolates hit him on the chest and rolled on the ground, having been flung with some force.

"Eat the damned things yourself, you rascal," growled his cousin.

Shanmugam sat there stunned for a while. His lips, defying his control, quivered. He tried to restrain his eyes from tearing up. He opened his mouth slightly and breathed in and out twice or thrice. No one around moved. The younger sister sat staring at him, shocked out of her wits. The elder sister pretended to be engrossed in The Illustrated Weekly and hid her face behind the magazine. Periamma's anger was evident from the manner in which she collected the coffee cups and stormed back into the kitchen.

Periappa gave a small smile. Pursed his lips and let out a peculiar whistle. Even though it was obvious he was seething, he managed to crack a joke in an attempt to ease the tension and cool things down. While Shanmugam somehow managed to smile at the wisecrack, it was tinged with a bit of shame at the insult.

Why not go out for a short walk? The day's good cheer had been totally destroyed. Even if it could not be reclaimed, he felt a semblance of normalcy would at least be welcome.

He thought back to what he had done wrong – that he did not send the newspaper to his cousin as soon as he was told? Or sending the sweets with his sister-in-law instead of taking them up himself? Whatever it was, none of it was deliberate. Perhaps he had not bothered to think it through either due to ignorance of niceties or in a rush of enthusiasm. Still, he felt he did not deserve this insult.

"Visalam, didn't you say we needed coffee?" enquired Periappa.

"Yes, I did. And we also need sugar."

It was kind of comforting walking with Periappa with a rolled-up cloth bag in his left hand. He kept talking of various matters throughout their stroll. They were all about how they have been disappointed with their son, the issues he had caused them, the slights he had inflicted and the problems he had created.

After dinner that night too, the conversation continued. In the course of it, Periappa suggested, "Go and lie down if you're feeling sleepy. It's already quite late."

He didn't feel like sleeping.

As the night progressed, a cool wind began blowing. The pesky mosquitoes had completed their nightly raid. Covering himself tightly with a shawl, Periappa said, "Come, let's go and have a cup of tea."

They shut the front door and went out. There was no one else on the streets. The tea-stall owner greeted Periappa warmly. The soot-stained clock on the wall struck two. They came back home and sat on the porch.

"After our mother's passing, Ayya married my chithi. My brother and I spent most of our time at our aunt's house in Krishnankoil. Ayya would come there on Friday evenings and take us back home. Chithi didn't like having us around. It was obvious to Ayya also, but he would ignore it for most of the time. Sometimes he would really lay into her for our sake. Your father Ramaswamy was just a little kid then. When we returned to Krishnankoil, our aunt would invariably ask, 'Did that woman give you anything to eat at all?' Ayya would also look in whenever he happened to be in those parts. He'd bring us some snacks or press a small coin or two in our hands. You should have heard our aunt start her litany of complaints about Chithi every time he landed there. Sometimes we would feel sorry for him. It was then that I ran away from home and joined a drama company.

"If our troupe was performing near Thirunelveli, I'd look in on them.

"At one time, the company was playing at Trivandrum. I had a day off. I caught a ride to Nagercoil and walked all the way up to the Kurungulam turn-off. Night was falling and all I had with me was my fare back to Trivandrum. I got scared that Chithi would revile me for not having brought any money. So I just lay down on the parapet wall of the bridge for a very long time. The night passed and I caught a ride with some carts proceeding to the market early the next morning and returned to Trivandrum.

"The next time I returned to our village, Ayya had passed away…

"Ayya was very keen to visit Palani and Thiruparankundram. I too wanted to take him to those temple towns. But that wish forever remained unfulfilled."

Despite it being a forty-year-old tale, the pain in Periappa's voice still seemed fresh. Perhaps he was only now rummaging through his repository of old memories. He went on relating more stories and reminiscences. It was obvious that Periappa had experienced life in all its facets. Shanmugam's respect for the man grew manifold. He felt proud and slightly envious at the same time.

As dawn broke, the city woke up. Sounds of human activity began to be heard. Sound of the bicycle bell heralded the milkman's arrival. Periamma woke up when he went in to fetch the milk bowl.

"Did you get any sleep at all last night?"

Shanmugam ensured that the hot water cauldron was filled. He brought in loads of water from the tap and filled the huge vessel.

Everyone in that household took their bath in hot water. Shanmugam did not feel cleansed if he bathed using a bucket and a mug. He therefore went to the well, pulled up several buckets of water and poured them all over himself. The smarting in his eyes ceased and he felt totally fresh. As he came in towelling his head, Periappa was seated on the cot drinking his coffee.

"Hey Shanmugam, why didn't you give the cow a bath while you were at it?" he joked.

He went to the University, gave them the completed form to receive his B.A. Certificate in absentia along with the receipt for the necessary fees that he had paid to State Bank of India, then proceeded to Egmore railway station and booked his return ticket home for the next day.

Periappa did not relish his act of buying the return ticket without consulting him.

He said his goodbyes to everybody including his annan, from whom the leave-taking resembled bidding farewell to a wall. While seeing him off, Periamma cautioned him, "Don't tell anyone at home of whatever transpired here."

He has not informed anyone in his house of these events. And in these three years, Annan has visited them once and Periappa twice. He interacted normally with everyone during his visits. In spite of him reminding Periappa when he was returning to Chennai, nothing has transpired so far. He was clueless of where things had gone wrong.

He just couldn't believe that it was beyond Periapppa's ability. If so, why hadn't he arranged for a job yet?

There was just one incident.

In 1967, the party Periappa was affiliated with came to power with a thumping majority.

All the party orators who had rendered themselves hoarse addressing their 'brothers and sisters' and 'fellow countrymen' throughout the State, celebrated the results for a whole year by organising congratulatory and thanksgiving meetings. After two years had rolled by, murmurs of dissent were becoming louder by the day.

Periappa happened to be visiting them at that time. During the course of a conversation, Shanmugam asked him,

"What happened to all your party spokesmen's big talk about the common man? Your partymen had said that the current inequality between the haves and the have-nots will disappear…why should only the rich man's child be able to get into medical college? 'We'll ensure that everybody will have a fair crack at such opportunities,' they said. What happened now? Can an ordinary man afford to pay thirty thousand rupees for a medical seat?"

Periappa replied. "All that is election talk. There will be exceptions."

"Then how come, within these two years, our M.L.A. has managed to acquire a rice mill, three taxis, a palatial house and a cinema theatre in Thuvarankadu? You yourself know that the fellow was previously employed in the Malaria Eradication Department at a salary of four hundred rupees and only owned a house worth two thousand rupees...how did this happen?"

"You know that the Congresswallahs also indulged in corruption."

"What are you saying, Periappa? Did Kunjan Nadar do it? Was T. S. Ramasamy Pillai corrupt? How about Nathaniel or Nesamani? Assuming the Congress guys were corrupt, do two wrongs make a right? Didn't you project yourselves as the 'party with a difference'?"

The whole of that day Periappa kept to himself, pondering over something. That could well be the reason.

But what was remarkable was that Appa had still not given up hope.

# 3

It has been rightly said that there's many a slip between the cup and the lip.

A temporary position became available at the Thovalai Panchayat Office. Someone was proceeding on maternity leave. Though the job was said to be for just two months, it would most likely be extended up to six months. The pay was around three hundred and sixty rupees. Every unemployed person in the District was talking of nothing else. Many were attempting to bring influence to bear via their M.L.A. or other bigwigs.

Shanmugam happened to mention this casually to Madasami annan during the course of a conversation.

It turned out that the President of the Panchayat Union and Madasami annan had studied together in High School. At one point in time, while Madasami annan had sold his gold ring to finance a meeting addressed by Periyar, the Union President had used a corner of the same grounds to set up a temporary shrine for their village deity Sudalai Madan and collect contributions from the faithful in the crowd.

After switching several parties along the way, depending upon which way the wind was blowing, he had now reached the exalted position of President of the Panchayat Union. Madasami annan had often made fun of this man's career progression.

One evening, when they were chatting on the parapet wall of the bridge, Madasami annan took him along to the President's house. They walked all the way and, during the entire journey, Madasami annan kept grousing. "Mind you, I'm coming along just for your sake. Otherwise, I have no wish to meet this son of a bitch. Ten years ago, he was nothing but a briefless lawyer, willing to work for a cup of coffee and a vadai. And look at him now, a bloody VIP! My arse! Whenever the Minister visits these parts, he stays at this fellow's house. When he was elected Union President, our people organised a meeting to felicitate him on his win and I was asked to speak on the occasion. Imagine the irony. I, who talk about Periyar and Annadurai, was made to speak in praise of this swine."

Madasami annan received a rousing reception at the President's house. He was offered coffee and snacks. "Of course anne, anything for you," he was promised effusively. Shanmugam's name and address was duly noted down. But the story ended on a familiar note. The job ultimately went to the son of the landlord in the neighbouring village who had paid three months' salary as a 'gift'. Where would Appa find the money for such offerings?

It was while he was in this disheartened state of mind that Iyer from Bombay came to Nagercoil after a long gap. Iyer owned a palatial house in Nagercoil. There was a stone porch some four feet high and five feet across, abutting the street. The house stretched endlessly inside. In their capacity as tenant farmers, Shanmugam had occasionally visited this house along with his father to deliver the landowner's share of the yield.

Iyer's uncle Periasami was over six feet tall and fair complexioned. As soon as he saw the cart containing over 20 sacks of rice roll into his courtyard, his first question would be, "Have you brought aval?" The sack containing the aval must be first unloaded and taken into the house. Appa would take off his turban, hold it in his hand, sit down on the floor and ask, "Sami, let me have some snuff."

Periasami was known to be very strict. He was over sixty years of age, but there was hardly an inch of spare flesh on his frame or any stoop in his bearing, the common signs of aging. He still retained all his original teeth even though his hair had turned totally white. His voice had a majestic timbre to it.

He was a B.A. graduate of his days and had been the manager in a local bank. Mistakenly believing chests filled with dark cinders to be tea leaves, he had sanctioned a loan to a client. As a result he had had to pay up an amount of ten thousand rupees, resign from his job and come back home some forty years ago. He never married. Having willed all his lands and possessions to his sisters after his time, he was leading a stress-free life.

Even though he was in the habit of loudly complaining about the yield and the quality, Periasami was, in reality, a softie.

Once the bullocks were unhitched, Appa, Shanmugam and the cart man would be served tall glasses of buttermilk. They had to drink it carefully, holding the glass high over their mouths ensuring it did not make any contact with their lips and, when empty, rinse it thoroughly and place it upside down on the floor. It seemed that to Appa and the cart driver, this was perfectly normal and in no way strange or demeaning, but not to Shanmugam.

On one occasion Shanmugam had gone there to announce that their share of the grain was arriving the next Friday. He preferred to stand while delivering the message rather than sit down on the ground. Periasami, noisily inhaling snuff, asked him to sit down on the cot. It did feel odd to sit on the cot and to leave the coffee tumbler unwashed behind him.

Whenever he spoke to Madasami annan, he felt a surge of murderous rage against all Brahmins which made him want to cut off every one of their top knots and chop off all their sacred threads. However, Periasami's attitude and behaviour evoked a kind of respect within him.

A Chettiar was engaged to measure the grain and re-bag them after removing the unripe portions. By the time he finishes, the twenty sacks of rice would have shrunk to fourteen. On top of that, he had to be given a 25 kilograms sack of grain as payment for his efforts. The Chettiar, in the belief that he was doing Periasami a huge favour, would keep packing and stuffing the measure with every ounce of his strength and vigour.

At one stage, Appa grew very frustrated and, unable to contain himself, burst out – "Sami, why do you condone such a sinful act? We labour and sweat it out for a full six months to be able to end up with at least two sacks of grain."

"What are you talking about Ramaswamy?" enquired a perplexed Periasami.

"Sami, you see what's going on here. You see how he is measuring? Even according to the government, a sack containing fourteen measures of rice would weigh only fifty-eight kilos. I dare him to weigh any one of these sacks…if even one of them weighs less than sixty-two kilos, I am willing to strip and walk back home in just my loincloth…"

The Chettiar was incensed.

"Sami, you can see for yourself that some of the grain is not ripe enough and there's dirt and worm castings."

"Unripe? Are you joking? The rice from Kurungulam is as good as gold dust and you know it! You're just finding fault for nothing."

"All right, Ramaswamy. Take it easy. Listen Chettiar, weigh justly and without bias…at my age I don't need a hardworking farmer's curse on my head. Why should I cheat him and to what end?"

"That's not it, sami…"

"Just do as you are told."

Occasionally, when the yield was low or disease affected the crops, he would instruct Chettiar to go easy on the measurements. Appa had been working their land for over thirty years now. During that time, Periasami never once insisted on increasing their agreed share of the yield or found fault with any other matter. Appa also took along with him plantains, greens, okra and whatever vegetables he grew on their property. They wouldn't complain if he chose to plant lentils or pulses in the summer. And he would ensure that they received their due share of these crops as well.

At least Periasami knew where their lands lay. Iyer had no clue about it at all.

He would show up with his family once every two or three years. When they heard about his arrival, they would send bunches of tender coconuts and ice apples for the entire family. Iyer turned out to be as naïve as Periasami. Shanmugam had met Iyer a long time ago while he was still a small boy.

When he came to Nagercoil for his April holidays, Appa had taken Shanmugam along with him. Appa and Iyer were of the same age. But Appa still addressed him as 'sami'. He would also take off his turban and hold it in his hand. He would only sit on the ground in his presence.

"Who's this Ramaswamy? Your son? Have you finished your studies?"

"I've completed my B.A., sami."

"When did you pass out?"

"In sixty-eight."

"Sami, please do something and arrange a job for him. We've tried everything here."

"What were you doing for the last three years? You could have dropped me a line earlier. Don't you have any sense? In the current situation, will either of us find a job in this State?"

"That's why I brought him along to meet you, sami…"

"You should be prepared to do any job that's offered to you. You need to have your wits about you to survive in Bombay. You can't come over there and start complaining about the food, the accommodation or that you miss your mother."

"He won't do all that, sami."

"Then, do this…come to Bombay after August 15th. Bring two trousers and two shirts, some four hundred rupees to support yourself for two months. I'll give you my address. Come and see me there. You can't stay with me, of course. Do you have any acquaintance living in Bombay?"

"Our Mookaiyah's son is there…in the military."

"That's good then. Write to him about your staying arrangements. I'll fix you up somewhere."

Iyer's words sounded credible. A straightforward person like him would never give him false hopes. He somehow felt confident that Iyer could do it. He would stay the first few days with Sundar annan, who was in the Navy, and then look around for suitable quarters of his own.

When they were returning home, Shanmugam felt as though he had already secured a job in Bombay.

—

Madras-Dadar Express. Will it take him all the way to Bombay? Even though the doubt lingered at the time of booking his ticket, he entered the train quite confidently. It was a three-tier sleeper coach. To be on the safe side, he made enquiries with a few other passengers on the train also.

Unlike his trip to Chennai, the names of the various stations that passed by appeared rather strange. Arakkonam, Renigunta, Guntakal…the names on the signboards were written in English, Hindi and the local language. The last resembled Tamil but with unfamiliar swirls and curlicues… Kannada maybe, or Telugu. Some names sounded unusual and he wondered how they were pronounced in English. Vadi, Gooty, Yerraguntla…

The towns differed. So did their attributes, the construction of the houses, ploughs, carriages, facial features of people, their dresses…

Some men wore turbans made out of long twisted dhotis while many wore Gandhi caps. Shanmugam had earlier been under the impression that anyone who wore a cap was a Muslim. In fact, he had his doubts about Jawaharlal Nehru on this score as well.

Women wore white bangles stacked up to their elbows. They sported large silver rings on their ears. They had on blouses that were open at the back and had glass pieces sewn on in the front. At some places, the women wore their saris in the typical style used by men, with the drape going between their legs. Women in his village would attend nature's calls standing upright with their legs spread apart, away from the public eye. He was unsure how these women managed to do their business.

The taste of water differed from place to place.

Since it was a broad-gauge compartment, Shanmugam had been allotted a single seat next to a window. It let him feel the blowing wind, look out at the scenery and daydream with his hands supporting his chin.

The rest of the compartment was occupied by a Gujarati family. Perhaps they had settled down in Chennai. They spoke good Tamil. Family arguments were however conducted in Gujarati in which the words 'che' and 'cho' kept occurring repeatedly. They had brought food in huge aluminium containers. Most of their time was spent eating, using both their hands for the purpose, and generously littering the inside of the compartment. He spent his time watching their activities, looking out at the passing scenery, and pondering with his eyes closed.

This time when he came to Chennai to board his train to Bombay, he did not stay at his Periappa's house. One of his college-mates was staying at a lodge in Pycrofts Road. He travelled to Chennai only after receiving confirmation that he could stay with him.

He bought his ticket to Bombay on arrival at Chennai. The ticket was for four days hence. During that period, he dropped in on his Periappa one morning. It was around ten thirty. They were obviously not expecting him. Periappa, clad only in a towel, was anointing himself with oil preparing for his bath. His shock at suddenly seeing Shanmugam at his doorstep was evident. His face brightened and his normal playful nature quickly asserted itself.

"Come in...why are you standing in the doorway?"

"Who're you talking to?" asked Periamma from inside the house.

"Come out and see for yourself. It's your brother-in-law's son."

Periamma was surprised to see him. "Hello, Shanmugam. When did you arrive?"

That's when Periappa noticed. "Where's your luggage? Is it in the taxi?"

"I…I arrived the day before yesterday."

"Where are you staying?"

"At Triplicane…in a lodge with a friend."

"Did you hear him? It's been three days since he arrived. He's staying at a lodge."

Periamma kept mum. There was silence for a beat. He felt scared. "Wait. Let me go and take my bath."

Periappa left to take his bath. Periamma returned to the kitchen. He began leafing through the Kumudam magazine that was lying on the table.

Periappa returned from his bath, leaving behind a trail of the heady aroma of sandalwood soap. Having towelled his head dry, he stood facing a corner of the room and changed into a dhoti. He then sat down on the cot. He dusted his feet against each other and hoisted them up. Beneath the dhoti, his feet appeared clean and shiny. His toenails were trimmed neatly. There were no blisters or cracks on his feet. The toenails were gleaming. Appa's feet were not like these at all. He had ingrown toenails which were discoloured and misshapen. Working constantly in the dirt and mud had caused his feet to develop huge blisters and cracks. Shanmugam had never once in his life seen his father wear slippers.

"Mmmm…so, you arrived three days ago?" He looked up at his face. Age seemed to have caught up with him. There were more lines on his face now. He had apparently lost a few teeth as well.

"Mmmm…have you got a job? Or are you here for an interview?"

"No…I am on my way to Bombay."

"Have you got a job there?"

"No…I need to look for one when I get there."

"Do you have to go that far away?"

"I agree it's very far…but I've no other option. Either I need to run very far away or else commit suicide. Since I lack the courage to die, I choose to run." As he said these words, Shanmugam's voice trembled with emotion. Periappa's face too changed. He looked down at the floor for a while.

"Mmmm…all right. Since you're already here, stay with us for a month at least. Check out of the lodge and come home. We'll give it a shot."

Very firmly, Shanmugam said, "No, Periappa. I've made up my mind. I'm going to Bombay."

Despite being asked to stay for lunch, he didn't accept. He could see they were a little hurt by his behaviour. However, he was determined and steadfast. He hadn't gone to see them of his own volition either. Both Appa and Amma had repeatedly insisted that he do so. "Just drop in and say hello. Who knows when you'll come back and who knows which of us will be around when you return."

Even though he told them he'd visit them again the next day, he had no intention of doing so. And he wasn't feeling particularly fraternal towards his brother or sisters either.

A strong feeling of resolve enveloped him. He needed to get to Bombay and secure a job. He would work tirelessly. He'd return a wealthy man. So many stories – he recalled many other incidents of people pulling themselves out of insufferable poverty by sheer hard work and determination.

During the rest of his stay in Chennai, as he went around the city, he felt highly envious of all those who were coming and going, proceeding to their places of work, carrying on their trade or business. When so many of them have found employment here and are able to earn a living, why did he have to flee so far away for his livelihood?

Shanmugam looked around at the people in the compartment. None of them was travelling for pleasure. There were those returning from their hometowns, those in search of employment, a few visiting relatives, others returning from a familial visit, those on holiday, married couples wishing to spread their wings, businessmen…

He couldn't even begin to imagine what Bombay would look like. It was described as a bustling metropolis. It had been classified as the seventh largest city in the world. He had been in similar awe of Chennai before he visited it. It was only after making it to the city did he realise how alien the capital was to the rest of Tamil Nadu. If Chennai had presented that image, what would Bombay be like? He had heard horror stories from several persons. The fears they engendered were still fresh in his mind.

The Hindi he had learnt up to Grade XI –

Yeh kya hai?
Yeh kalam hai!
Woh kya hai?
Woh kamal hai!

Laddu: feminine gender; Banana: masculine gender. Strange rules of grammar!

His English was not all that great either. Writing a five-page essay on 'India's Population Problem' was one thing; trying to talk about it conversationally was altogether different. Not having had the need to speak before, he had to put his fluency to test now.

Apart from this, he had no clue what the local language, Marathi, even sounded like. He had plenty of apprehensions about the Shiv Sena: Shiv Sainiks beat up elderly Tamils at Matunga; Tamil women harassed; Shops of Tamilians broken into and vandalised; Policemen dragged into a house at Dharavi and killed; Countless murders…

—

The morning dawned at Poona.

He brushed his teeth and bought himself a breakfast of pooris and potato curry for a rupee. The pooris were rubbery and utterly tasteless. Was this a harbinger of things to come? He recalled the days when he used to savour pooris and potato curry or chapatti and korma at restaurants like Ashok Bhavan and Arya Bhavan. The very thought constricted his throat and made swallowing the rubbery mess even more difficult. As he and some of his fellow-passengers were having their breakfast, there were a number of youngsters around with outstretched arms begging for hand-outs. A few passengers gobbled up their food in a hurry to avoid them, a few turned their faces away and continued eating while some shooed them away roughly.

It had been seven days since he left home. But it somehow seemed longer. He began wondering when he would be able to return home to his family and friends again. The very thought that once he secured a job he wouldn't be able to procure leave for a whole year to go back home terrified him. He was also worried whether Sundar annan would be at the station to receive him. He had written to him ten days ago.

Would the letter have reached him by now? Of course, he had his address with him. And he remembered the directions provided by Sundar annan's father.

"It is a very old-style building…there would be pigeons roosting all over it…there would be people selling apples and oranges outside the building. There are two or three buses going from there to Devi Nagar. Twenty paise is the bus fare. There will be a lot of buildings all around. If you get down and enquire, someone will direct you."

These were the directions to his house from Victoria Terminus, the historic train station in Bombay. 'But how do I go there from Dadar? We'll see when we get there,' he decided.

The train left Poona behind. Khandala, Lonavala…there were a lot of tunnels through mountains. As he pressed his face to the window and peered out, he could see the train entering a tunnel like a serpent sliding headfirst into its burrow. They passed Karjat and came to Kalyan. A number of passengers disembarked. Next stop Dadar, they said.

Shanmugam collected his comb, towel, bedspread and a magazine strewn around and packed them into his suitcase. He changed from his lungi and dirty shirt into a clean shirt and trousers. He kept his ticket carefully in his pocket. For the twenty-sixth time, he checked to confirm that the file containing his certificates was safe within the suitcase. From his secret cache, he withdrew twenty rupees and transferred it to his trouser pocket.

The train was approaching the station. Its speed reduced considerably. By the time he could turn around, it had crawled into the burrow-like platform and come to a stop. The signboard on the platform read 'Dadar' in English also.

He felt disoriented as if the day, the date and the directions had all gone awry. People rushed out in a flood of humanity.

Trunks, holdalls, suitcases, cardboard cartons, sacks, backpacks, bedrolls, cloth bags. Men in a variety of dhotis, tight trousers, jeans, lungis. Women in saris, silks, churidars, salwar kameez…

It was teeming with taxis outside the terminal. And a few jeeps, vans and cars. The Sikh taxi-drivers in their turbans and beards were welcoming each visitor as though they were guests at a wedding.

Shanmugam's suitcase was not all that heavy. In addition, he carried a cardboard carton with stuff that Sundar annan's parents had sent for him. He followed Sundar annan, keeping his green-striped shirt in view at all times. They took a local train to Victoria Terminus and had a meal at the railway restaurant on the second floor of the terminus building. As he ate what was put before him, he seriously contemplated taking the evening train home. Four pooris, two small clumps of rice, a cup of watery dal, a cup of some indeterminate gravy (sambar?), a spoonful of a dry curry made of potatoes and brinjal, a small quantity of stringy beans, a piece of pickle and half a papadum. The charge for all this was two rupees. Back home, he could have had his fill for five annas or thirty-one paise. He did not know how long he could survive on this so-called 'Rice Plate'. After drinking a lot of water, he achieved some semblance of a full stomach.

They took the No. 3 bus from there and reached the Devi Nagar bus stop. They walked home from there.

Sundar annan kept pointing out buildings and landmarks throughout the journey. "This is V.T. When you come out you'll see another building on its side. That's the Bombay Municipality building. Next to it is the Times of India newspaper office. If we go to the bus stop opposite that building, we can board either No. 3 or No. 45. Both end up at Devi Nagar bus terminus. You can also take No. 103, but it goes up to R.C. Church. We don't need to go that far. At the last turning we can get off at the Afghan Church. I'll show it to you on the way and if we walk to the right, we'll reach Devi Nagar."

The bus stopped at Devi Nagar terminus. "We're getting off at the very last stop just for your sake. Look around and take a careful note of everything. We should have got off at the previous stop. Be sure to remember all the landmarks. Do you see that 11-storey building painted black? That's the T.I.F.R. – Tata Institute of Fundamental Research. The building opposite it is also theirs. I'll take you there one of these days. If you go along this road and turn right, there's the Central School on your right and Smita Market on the left. It's still under construction. Take the next road and go straight, the first house on the fourth row—Block 'F', the first house on the ground floor. When you are here on your own, remember to walk briskly and purposefully. Don't dawdle. The entire premise is defence area. If you seem to be loitering or unsure of where you're headed, you may be stopped and questioned… who you are, why you are here, who you are visiting and so on. Got it?"

Sundar annan's house was spacious. As soon as you entered, there was a balcony and then two rooms. There was a kitchen at the back, a storeroom, bath and toilet. A Punjabi family was occupying the first room and the storeroom. Sundar annan's family was using the second room and the kitchen. Since his wife had gone to her maternal home for her delivery, Sundar annan was currently on his own.

"You can stay here for two months. My wife and baby will be here thereafter. We can look around for a room somewhere nearby. I don't cook often. I don't care for cooking and dish washing. Mornings I make do with bread, butter and jam. You can get some yourself. Or else, I'll get them for you from the Navy Canteen Stores. Everything is cheap there. Other stuff like soap and toothpaste can also be procured from there. All right, take a bath and get some rest now. I'm off to Angre and will be back by five o' clock. I'll then take you around and show you the sights. Since tomorrow is Sunday, we'll go and meet Iyer, all right?"

# 4

He had been in Bombay for a month now. And he had gone up and down several offices and homes armed with Iyer's letters of introduction and slips containing addresses.

Each one had a different reason to turn him down: Maharashtra is experiencing a severe drought and famine this year; there is a forty percent electricity cut in force; we've only recently laid off several employees in our organisation; we've no plans of recruiting a South Indian in our company at present.

They asked for qualifications he didn't possess. 'Come back after a week, just in case,' some said. Having taken the completed application form a few would send him off with the words 'don't call us, we'll call you.'

He placed an advertisement in the Times of India, spending eight rupees and thirty paise: 24-year old recent B.A. graduate (Second Class) seeks employment. He received ten to twelve responses. They called him for interviews. He went to each one of them with great expectations.

Typewriting/shorthand? Sorry, I don't know either.

Debit/Credit? No idea at all.

Previous experience? Nil.

Knowledge of the local language? Zero.

Beyond this, no one appeared willing to offer him a job even for two hundred rupees a month. He would recount his experiences at the end of each day to Sundar annan.

He carried a letter of recommendation to Mr. S. K. Singh of R.K. Edward & Co. Pvt. Ltd. on Arthur Bunder Road, only to be informed that Mr. Singh had passed away two months ago.

He met Mr. Ganesan of Premier Alloys on Meadow Street who sat him down, offered him a cup of coffee and enquired with great concern about his family circumstances, only to finally admit that he had no say in recruitment matters, and then send him on his way with a diary.

He was about to meet the Chartered Accountant, Mr. Sthanukrishnan, at Sir Phiroze Shah Mehta Road and inadvertently walked into his office without knocking or prior announcement. He faced a barrage of the choicest abuses in chaste English.

Maniklal Mehta at Marine Lines, who ran an agency for winding machinery, and who spoke colloquial Tamil because of his frequent visits to Coimbatore, strung him along for days on end.

Every time Sundar annan consoled him, saying, "Don't be disheartened. You're sure to land a job soon…be strong." his grief threatened to overwhelm him.

His cash reserves were dwindling alarmingly fast day by day. Even though he did not have to pay rent for his accommodation, transportation and food cost a minimum of five rupees each day. At this rate he would last one more month. What would happen thereafter?

Could he write home asking for more money? Should he go back home? But, where's the money for the return fare?

If he went back with his tail between his legs, how would he face all those at home who had high expectations of him?

He made sure to visit Iyer at least three or four times a week. Having had tiffin and coffee at their place, on his way back to the railway station holding a fresh bunch of letters and address slips, he looked up at the sky and tried to swallow his disappointment.

Once, during a conversation with Sundar annan, he said, "I'm determined not to go back without securing a job. I'd rather drown myself in the Arabian Sea instead." Sundar annan became furious at this. He began railing at him, "How dare you speak such things in front of me?" But his situation showed no signs of improvement.

Once, even Iyer felt frustrated enough to comment, "How is it that nothing seems to work out for you? In the past, my recommendations would take ten days at the most to fetch a job. But, don't worry. Trust in God. I'll see to it that you're properly slotted in somewhere."

There would be days when he would have no one to meet. Since there was nothing else for him to do, he would use the train pass that he had bought for the Churchgate to Andheri line, to go on an exploratory trip.

Some days he would catch the Andheri local, travel up to its final destination and return by the same train, looking out of the window, watching the passengers getting on or off, thinking his own private thoughts, being jostled and pushed around by the crowd.

At other times, he would get off at Bombay Central and, carefully noting his route, walk till his feet hurt. Sometimes Dadar, sometimes Khar Road.

Life was very fast in Bombay. It was impossible to walk swinging one's arms in a carefree manner. There was considerable crowding and pushing and shoving everywhere. The ladies did not seem fazed by this. For their part, they too pushed and muscled their way into trains and buses. They stood unconcernedly holding the overhead straps in the buses, showing off their smooth-shaven armpits. Or else, they sat with their legs spread wide apart in short skirts that didn't quite reach their knees.

Having been used to ogling women bathing at the river in his village, this blasé display of flesh overwhelmed Shanmugam.

He gazed at the vegetable vendors, the fruit sellers, the utensil and cloth shops spread out at the edge of the road, the cows lounging around…There seemed to be bus, lorry, taxi, car, smoke, dust and noise everywhere.

There were a number of huts all along the pavements—roofed with polythene sheets, hessian sacks, tin sheets, cardboard pieces, rags, reed mats, children defecating outside the huts, women washing utensils, men sleeping off their overindulgence of arrack that morning.

The food at every eating house tasted the same. There was no difference at all between their 'Rice Plates'. The same smells assailed the nostrils whenever one entered any of these establishments.

He sometimes wondered how he would survive this city even if he did manage to find a job here.

Sometimes Shanmugam would sit on the retaining wall at Nariman Point and stare at the sea. To his eyes, the sea here wasn't as beautiful as the one at Kanyakumari. It looked crude and obscene like an aborted foetus. That was when the tide was in. When the tide was out, the sight was even more horrendous. The city's waste, effluence, garbage, oil slicks – all produced a stinking smell that was sure to damage the mental and physical wellbeing of any person. Tender coconut shells, corncobs, broken plastic items, dried flower garlands were among the rubbish that floated out to the sea.

Sometimes he would go to Horniman Circle or to the Central Library next to INS Angre where Sundar annan worked. Tall steps, imposing pillars, dark alcoves where pigeons roosted, pigeon droppings, their smell, darkness, stacks of old books and magazines. He would catch up on a week-old Dinamani here.

Suddenly one day Sundar annan made a happy announcement. He had heard from his colleague, Karve that there was a temporary vacancy at the Collector's Office in the old Customs House and that Karve had arranged for Shanmugam to get it. Shanmugam presented himself at ten in the morning the next day and met a Mr. Gonsalvez, who apparently knew a few words of Malayalam. The section was meant for ex-servicemen. He agreed to let Shanmugam work there for a few days. But there would be no formal appointment letter to that effect.

They gave him a file containing over a thousand addresses along with a stack of envelopes and told him to get to work.

The envelopes contained the words 'Flag Day Invitation' prominently in the front. He transcribed addresses every day till his fingers cramped up. He'd leave his seat only to take a leak or to have lunch.

Every morning Major Mamunkar would arrive by the Deccan Queen and appear at the office at 10.45 a.m., carrying a leather bag in one hand and a folding blue canvas stool in the other. He would leave at 4.30 p.m. to catch the evening train back. He would presumably be in Poona by around eight p.m.

Gonsalvez basically handled everything in the office. There were three female clerks who conversed among themselves mostly in Marathi, occasionally in Hindi and very rarely in English. They did everything together. None of them bothered to include Shanmugam in their conversations or even toss a smile in his direction. Several aged persons in old military uniforms came to the department to clarify whatever doubts and queries they had.

After four days of addressing envelopes, he was asked to collect boxes from a large room situated opposite the office which was used as a storeroom. The boxes, marked 'Flag Day – Please Donate' were to be bunched together numerically into parcels of ten, and a note made in a ledger.

After the signs were printed and affixed to the boxes, and Shanmugam had assembled them in order, the boxes were loaded onto a jeep and taken away. All this activity took another four days. While this was going on, he observed that a girl in a salwar kameez was seated at his old spot and was busily writing something. Her free and easy manner and the way she spoke to the bald coot with the missing teeth seemed to suggest she was his daughter.

When all the boxes had been dispatched, Shanmugam went and stood beside Gonsalvez.

"All done?"

"Yes sir."

Gonsalvez called the cashier over and instructed him to pay Shanmugam forty-five rupees as wages for nine days.

After deducting twenty paise towards the cost of a revenue stamp and a refugee relief stamp, Shanmugam was paid his dues after he had signed the receipt. The new girl was unhurriedly transcribing addresses on another stack of envelopes.

He took his leave of Gonsalvez. He felt the rush of having drawn his first salary from the government of India. At the same time, he felt a sense of deprivation.

It was only four thirty. He decided to spend some time in that area and have his dinner before returning home. That made more sense than going back home straightaway and making a second trip for food later. He would rather go to bed hungry.

But the thought of food made him feel nauseous. The very idea of pooris sickened him. But when you compared six pooris to a cup of rice, pooris won the day for appeasing his appetite.

He had definitely lost weight since coming here. His trousers refused to stay up around his waist and kept slipping down. Unfortunately, his tailor back at the village had not fitted them with loops through which he could thread a belt. He had to fold the trouser around his waist to hold it in place.

Walking past the Lion Gate Council Hall, taking a turn near Regal Cinema he went towards the Gateway of India. This was familiar territory—the same statue of Chhatrapati Shivaji. The statue of Swami Vivekananda standing with his arms crossed across his chest. There was the Tajmahal Hotel and the Taj Intercontinental. The welcome arch constructed to welcome the eighth (or was it the ninth?) Prince of Wales. Benches built of beige and red stones dotted the area. He sat on one of them gazing out at the sea and the ships visible in the distance.

As evening fell, the sightseeing crowd grew large with first-time visitors to Bombay, long-time residents who had come to admire the view, lovers holding hands and newly married couples.

Night-time came creeping. It was December and slightly cold. The crowd had increased. A few sported pullovers.

'Bhaiyas' from UP threaded through the crowd, carrying aluminium basins the size of kettledrums harnessed to their necks. They hawked savoury snacks made out of gram, kept warm by pots containing burning coals, all the while yelling out, "Chana Jor Garam…" For some reason, everyone from UP was addressed as 'bhaiya': vegetable and fruit vendors, the milk seller, the handcart-puller, the person who sat under the shade of a tree and handed a looking glass for you to hold up while proceeding to give you a shave, the guy who operated the wheat mill…Everyone was addressed by their respective professions as 'milk bhaiya', 'vegetable bhaiya' and so on. On occasions, he has even heard Iyer refer to Nehru as 'bhaiya'.

Drinking water was being sold at five paise a glass; There was a popcorn seller, an ice-cream cart and people selling conch shells, bead necklaces, deer antlers and other handicraft products. The only thing missing was a large idol of a guardian deity for the piazza.

The ships at the distance had switched their lights on. He remembered what Sundar annan had told him about them. They were vessels waiting for a berth at the Bombay port and, sometimes, they waited for their turn upstream for ten to fifteen days at a stretch.

Shanmugam had a long-standing wish to sail on a ship. He had had this desire ever since he had read historical novels back home. How pleasant would it be to be afloat at sea surrounded by water on all sides? Apparently, there was a steamer service from Bombay to Goa. The scenic beauty of that trip was talked about highly. Once he got a job and began earning well, he would take a trip on a ship to Goa during his holidays. His stomach grumbled. Even though the thought of food was unpalatable, hunger pangs were incessant.

He would go and meet Iyer tomorrow. While returning, he would get off at Matunga Road, cross the over-bridge and eat at the Malayali mess on the second floor of a building at King's Circle. The place did not go in for frills like pooris, rice, gravy and accompaniments in separate bowls, but instead served a large helping of parboiled rice with fish curry. It cost just one rupee. If you wanted an additional side dish like fried fish, egg curry or yogurt, that would be another thirty paise.

Letters came regularly from home. Every one of them was a variation of the same message: Have you secured a job yet? Take care of yourself; Pass our regards to Sundaram Iyer; Harvesting season has begun; It's time now for spraying fertilizers.

It has been one and a half months since he made it to Bombay. He felt ashamed to admit that he had not yet succeeded in securing employment.

—

It was Christmas day. A public holiday. So Shanmugam went to meet Iyer.

"Come, Shanmugam. How are you doing?" There was a lilt in Iyer's tone as he greeted him. "Something has come up at last. You know Reay Road railway station, don't you? It's on the Harbour Line. From VT station there are trains for Kurla, Mankhurd, Bandra and Chembur on platforms 1 or 2. Masjid, Sandhurst Road, Dockyard Road, Reay Road... the fourth station. Get down there and ask for directions to Atlas Mills Compound. The company, R.H. Thompson, is inside that compound. Go in and ask for Mr. Dikmani – their Works Manager. Give him this letter. Don't talk to him about salary and stuff like that. If he asks you anything, just tell him to refer to me. Don't go this week. The First of this month is a Sunday, so go there on Monday."

He reverentially secreted the envelope Iyer handed to him. He also carefully memorised the address. He felt a little enthused. But also faintly sceptical. How many times had he ventured forth in this manner only to be disappointed at the end?

He had lunch with the Iyers that day, though it felt a little odd to sit alongside them and dine on equal footing. The dining table was set for everyone. Iyer took a few drops of water in his right hand, circled the food on his plate and, muttering some mantras, put three grains of the cooked rice into his mouth. Everyone then commenced eating.

Shanmugam was sure his appa wouldn't have sat alongside that family and eaten with them like an equal. He was used to sitting on the ground at Iyer's house. If he was given coffee or buttermilk, he would drink it with the glass held high over his mouth. Thereafter, as he held the tumbler out, a lady of the household would pour water over it and he would rinse and leave it upturned in a corner of the verandah.

Shanmugam remembered the times when Appa had taken his bullock-cart and spent days on end outside Iyer's house, running errands, helping with the shopping and doing miscellaneous chores during the latter's sister-in-law's wedding.

The bullocks had no issues with it at all. But humans? Appa has recounted several times how, at that wedding, he was consistently made to wait till all the portly Brahmins, awash with sweat, potbellies swaying and sacred threads fluttering, had finished their meals. He was then seated along with the musicians, the local barber and washerman and served his food. At such times, Shanmugam would wonder, 'This is how we treat field-hands at our household weddings. Does Appa feel the pinch then?'

"Go ahead, help yourself to some more sambar. Do you want another papadum?"

Shanmugam felt emotional. He ate his fill after a very long time. Every time he had visited the Iyers, he had never been sent away on an empty stomach. On that day however, when he was on his way back to Colaba, both his heart and stomach were full to the brim.

On the 2nd, he made his way to the company on Reay Road. All these days, he had only been to small establishments or to branch and head offices of firms, and had never visited a manufacturing concern before. He had only seen such establishments from the outside during his travels on local trains. Once, in Pokharan Road No. 2 in Thane, he had seen a few factories: Voltas, Inarco, W.G. Forge etc. There had also been some huge factories on his way to Thane: Godrej, Crompton Greaves, Guest Keen Williams and so on. He had also caught glimpses of a few huge mills within the city while travelling around in buses—Dawn Mills, Morarjee Mills, Kohinoor Mills–with their long smokestacks aggressively thrusting up as though posing a sexual challenge to the skies.

He assumed R.H. Thompson would be one such humongous factory, as he headed towards it. He got down at Reay Road railway station at 8.45 a.m. and came out onto the road to find both its sides lined with ramshackle huts constructed of pieces of rags. The stink of urine. Steaming piles of fresh human excrement everywhere. An unending stream of lorries.

A woman was scouring aluminium vessels using grit.

Another woman was busily beheading, gutting and cutting the tails off red mullets, which appeared pretty but were just so-so in taste.

A lady was seated outside her hut bathing, using a bucket of water and a tin mug for the purpose.

A fourth was seated on a wooden plank with her sari hitched up to her knees holding a child between her legs as it defecated. It passed a thin stream of yellow faecal matter as though afflicted with some sort of a stomach ailment.

A lot of the families appeared to be Muslims.

Rice was cooking in front of a hut, the steam making the lid on the pot dance. An idli seller was seated in front of another shack stacking seven or eight idlis on a plate and ladling sambar and chutney over them. A little girl, holding out a rupee note towards the vendor, was asking him for extra chutney. Two men were busy brushing their teeth while a third stood holding a cup of tea in one hand and a beedi in the other. Sewage frothed and foamed as it ran alongside the road like a canal.

When he asked for directions to the Atlas Mills Compound, he was shown a cave-like gate into which a large lorry was seen entering. The path inside was completely covered by litter, dead leaves and rubbish. There were four or five small workshops on either side. The ubiquitous drain ran through this compound too. Mamaji Industries, Saifee Electroplaters, Speedway Products and, finally, the fourth one, R.H. Thompson. A Gurkha watchman dressed in an outdated uniform of khaki trousers, shirt and a cap was outside the gate with a bamboo staff in his hand.

Upon showing the gurkha the letter Iyer had sent for Dikmani – God knows what he made of it – he was directed inside. A sofa stood inside, next to a cabin. An internal doorway led into the premises.

The Gurkha sounded a gong to signify that it was 9 o' clock.

Unsure of what to do, Shanmugam perched on the sofa and looked around in confusion. He could see plenty of wooden planks stacked inside. A few large wooden boxes lay around partially completed. He wondered if it was a timber shop.

As he was gazing around perplexedly, a fair, tall, thin man came and stood next to him.

"Yes?" asked the man with an insincere smile pasted on his face. "Please wait. Mr. Dikmani will be here shortly."

Perhaps there was another workspace beyond the area where the wooden articles were lying around. People were coming and going. From the Stores area, two men brought out a crate containing miscellaneous articles. He could also hear a stove hissing and the sound of cups and saucers rattling.

Everyone was served tea. Perhaps it was the practice of the firm to provide it. At a signal from the thin man, Shanmugam was also served a cup of tea. The heat of the drink scalded his tongue. The tang of ginger suffused it.

He heard a car come to a stop outside the premises. A tall, well-built man, dressed in a suit and tie walked in smartly carrying a briefcase. The sound of the activity inside the workshop ratcheted up a notch. This must be Mr. Dikmani.

As he walked into his cabin, Shanmugam could smell the faint scent of incense sticks and hear the muted hum of an air conditioner from inside the room.

The tall man went into the office room and came out after a while. Dikmani walked out of his office and went into the workplace. Shanmugam could hear the 'whirrr' of the saws, and 'thwack, thwack' of the cut wooden planks falling to the ground.

When Dikmani returned after a while, Shanmugam stood up. When he paused, he extended the envelope to him. He opened it and quickly glanced at the contents of the letter. He asked Shanmugam to follow him and entered his office again.

He did not invite Shanmugam to sit. He asked some general questions. He did not scrutinise the certificates. He pressed the intercom and said, "Mr. Acharya". The tall man came in.

"I'm asking him to come to work from Monday onwards. Accommodate him somewhere."

"Where do I fit him in?"

"Put him next to Raut."

Acharya looked at him strangely and walked out. He thanked Dikmani and came out. He could feel the heat in the air outside. He deferentially took his leave of Acharya and left the premises.

He went to Iyer's that evening and reported to him. "Good. Work hard and prove yourself. You don't have to come here regularly anymore. Come and see me only if you need something."

January the 8th was a day to remember for Shanmugam. That was the day he started his first job. He caught the No. 3 bus from Colaba, got off at Victoria Terminus, bought himself a season ticket, got on the Harbour Branch train and detrained at Reay Road. He reached his workplace before 9 o' clock. The others arrived one by one carrying a small handbag, holding a tiffin box tucked inside a cloth bag, slinging a shoulder bag or lugging a medical representative's bag.

Acharya arrived and handed the keys to the store and the office cabin. After they were opened, a woman came and swept the premises. A peon dusted the chairs and tables. The workday commenced.

In the packing section, where the semi-finished wooden boxes lay, there was a long table in which two persons sat facing a wall. Shanmugam joined them there as the third person. The man in one corner was S.C. Dele – Shivaji 'Chandu' Dele. Next to him was S.S. Raut – Sathyavan Shivaram Raut. Both were Maharashtrians.

Dele had a muster register and some red-coloured cards in front of him. He stacked the cards numerically and was noting the time on each of them. In front of Raut was an unopened register prominently labelled E.S.I.C.

No one seemed to be in a hurry to commence work.

The workmen who passed by looked curiously at the new hire. Tea was served after a short while. Then Shanmugam went and stood by Acharya who said a couple of words as though granting him a huge favour.

Preparing gate passes. Writing challans. Drawing up octroi invoices. Making labels for boxes ready for dispatch. Keeping track of incoming spares.

Ten days rolled by.

Dele was still busy marking attendance for the forty staff members, filling leave forms for the four or five employees who did not turn up the day before or completing yellow forms for those who arrived late or wished to leave early. The register marked E.S.I.C. continued to lie in front of Raut. If Dikmani was in, it would be open. At all other times it remained closed. Dikmani only spent a maximum of two to three hours daily at the workshop. Otherwise, it was Acharya who ran the show. He behaved like a spoilt child. Everyone either coddled him or cajoled him.

In the workshop, they assembled two types of machinery. Parts were procured from places like Ahmedabad, Navsari and Surendranagar as well as from small fabricators in Bombay and assembled here. They made textile winding machines. One was the Thompson Precision Winder consisting of six spindles and the other was the Thompson Coners made up of one hundred and twenty spindles.

It was a factory employing forty persons in all. As such, it came under the provisions of The Shops & Establishment Act. A board announced that Sundays were holidays, working hours were from 9 to 5.15 with a break between 1.00 and 1.30 for lunch and the salary date was the Seventh of each month.

Seven persons, including Acharya, made up the store and office staff. There were four bakers, one watchman, one supervisor, three erectors and two painters. The rest were all fabricators.

The factory itself contained the storeroom, Dikmani's cabin, baking section, assembly section, urinal, a wash area for cleaning one's hands and feet and a stand containing a pot with drinking water. No one seemed to have enough work to keep him occupied for eight hours except for Acharya. He seemed constantly busy bustling about, talking on the telephone, writing something, hailing everyone around.

Saturdays were half-days. The workshop was closed on Sundays and on other Bank holidays. Apart from the miscellaneous jobs, Shanmugam was also asked to prepare a price list for spare parts. That took another fifteen days. On the Seventh, he was paid a salary of one hundred and sixty-eight rupees for having worked twenty-four days.

He felt odd. He bought some sweets and went to meet Iyer. Stick around for six months and we shall see thereafter, he counselled.

The whole month of February had to be negotiated. He would have to manage for some time on two hundred and ten rupees per month. On a rough estimate, rent came to twenty-five, bus fare was ten rupees, season ticket was six, tea at the firm cost fifteen, twenty-five for breakfast, lunch cost thirty, dinner thirty-seven, eight rupees for oil, soap, toothpaste, inland letters and so on. If everything totalled one hundred and sixty, he could still save about fifty rupees. He would send it home.

If he pinched his personal spending a bit more, he could afford to purchase some new clothes for himself and put some aside towards travel expenses back home.

The very thought made him feel homesick.

# 5

Sound sleep evaded him at nights. Even the slightest noise was enough to rouse him from his slumber: the tap of the watchman's staff on the road as he made his rounds, the howl of a lone dog in memory of some long-forgotten yearning, the growl of the heavy truck painted olive green arriving late at night at the neighbouring garrison engineering workshop, the sound of the sardar clearing his throat in the house across...

Shanmugam would take every precaution before going to sleep. He had positioned his bed close to the wall in such a way that it would not be easily visible if anyone shone a torch through the ventilator windows at either the front or the back entrances. He also leaned a camp cot against the bed and spread a bed sheet over it to camouflage his presence.

He would return home late at night after dinner. Unnecessary usage of lights was avoided. A dim table lamp provided the required illumination. When he was ready to go to bed, he would hand over the key to the flat to Surve who would then lock the front door. He would latch the back door from the inside. In the mornings, Surve would unlock the door and hand him the key so that he could leave for work after locking up behind him.

This had become the standard protocol ever since Sundar annan left for his hometown on his annual leave. Rigorous checking was being carried out throughout Devi Nagar for illegal residents. Due to the severe shortage of accommodation, each apartment housed two families. If both were Navy personnel such sharing was permitted after submitting a written application and obtaining an official sanction. Civilians were totally barred. But still, several Malayali families and a few bachelors managed to stay there under the radar. It was to check such unauthorised occupation that the Naval Police had begun conducting surprise raids around midnight or at one o'clock in the mornings. The date and time of these sorties were closely guarded secrets.

Before he left, Sundar annan had repeatedly told Shanmugam and Surve, "If I was here, there would be no issues. I'd tell them he's my brother and has just arrived yesterday from our village. You better take care. Otherwise, by the time I return, they'd have leased the premises to someone else."

Surve was a scaredy-cat. The arrangement had been put in place only after consultations with him. If a sudden raid took place, he was to tell the raiding party that Sundaram had gone on leave, he'd taken away the house keys with him and there was no one inside the apartment.

Yet a silent fear festered in his mind and he couldn't help but wish Sundar annan would come back soon. But what if he brought his family back with him when he returned? Then Shanmugam would have no option but to move out within four or five days at the most. He would never get another place as comfortable as this for twenty-five rupees. In one sense, he had been so far cushioned against one of Bombay's most pressing problems. It was now time to venture forth and face reality.

As usual, Shanmugam had his dinner, came into the flat, arranged his bed, switched off the light and went to sleep.

His thoughts went back to his home. He then mulled over his work issues for a while. The weather had turned cool. He imagined having a girl next to him, keeping him warm while they had sex, and fell asleep with this pleasant thought.

There was a sudden banging on the door. He could hear the doors on all the eight buildings in the row being pounded in different rhythms. He also heard Surve open the door and the sound of voices inside the building. To Shanmugam's ears, his own breathing sounded as loud as a steam engine. There was the sound of the lock being rattled. A dim beam of torchlight slowly moved through the room's dark recesses. His heart beat as loud and fast as an express train. It was quiet after a while. He felt he had emerged unscathed from an ordeal. There was nothing more to fear, he thought. He thought wrong.

The next night, when he was sound asleep, he heard a scraping sound on the back door. It sounded like an urgent summons. He got up and, without switching on the light, tiptoed to the door and unlatched it.

"Hurry, get out of the back door...they're here again for checking."

As soon as the message registered, he slung a shirt over his shoulders and, grabbing a pair of trousers, rushed out barefoot into the darkness. He didn't bother buttoning his pants; instead, he held it up with both hands in his headlong rush.

By the time Surve noiselessly shut the back door and went to open the front door to the raiding party, Shanmugam had put on his shirt, buttoned up his trousers and reached the edge of the building.

Was it the same checking party that had come yesterday or a different one? Have they deliberately targeted the building for a second time in a row, or was this crew unaware that a check had already taken place yesterday? Will they merely check the front lock and move away? Or, will they come around to check the back door as well? If they did, wouldn't they notice that the back door was unlocked and grill Surve? So many questions.

He sensed the imminent danger of his position, lurking like a thief in the shadows. The very thought that there would be no escape if he got caught in the beams of the Naval Police's roving torchlights gave him the jitters.

He carefully crept to the edge of the building and peeked out. A police truck was parked two buildings away with all its lights switched off. Several policemen had entered the buildings and were pounding on doors. Thud, thud, thud. A few policemen stood guard outside; their cigarette-ends were glowing pinpoints in the darkness.

The moon was covered by clouds and so there was not much light. A bitter, cold wind was blowing. He reversed his direction, walked along the edges of the buildings, reached the last one, stood in the darkness at the border wall to the garrison workshop and carefully scanned the road opposite. He then entered the dense tree cover and walked through the darkness of the night.

This was the eastern border of Devi Nagar. There was no one around. He stood in the shaded darkness provided by two banyan trees waiting for his pulse to return to normal, and considered his next move. He decided to walk towards the bus stand and came to the main road. The place was deserted. He walked towards the bus terminus.

Vegetable and fruit carts stood shrouded in gunny sacks on the side of the road. Bhaiyas lay asleep under their carts on sacks topped with bedspreads, wrapped tightly in blankets against the cold.

Since the Tata Institute of Fundamental Research was situated on the western side of the road, the street from there till the

Afghan Church was properly paved, flanked on both sides by a six feet wide pavement constructed of stone slabs. The edges were lined with flowering laburnum trees.

Apart from the cold and darkness, there was nothing else around. Bathroom lights in some of the buildings around winked on and off. A jeep left the premises of the T.I.F.R., its tyres making a hissing noise as it sped past. That sound was the only diversion in an otherwise silent setting.

A large number of Telugu Kamathis–artisans and construction workers from Telangana–were lying asleep in front of the partially completed Smita Market. The size and shapes of some of the mounds wrapped in blankets seemed to suggest that husbands and wives were lying tightly in an intricate embrace inside those bundles.

A short distance away, some men were seated around a fire fuelled by dried leaves and rubbish. A few of them were smoking cheroots and the others were nodding off in their seated position. There was no conversation. God knows how long they had been sitting there silently, just warming their hands against the fire and tucking them back into their blankets.

A cold wind passed by. He shivered and went to squat by the fire. The man next to him lifted his head, looked at him and moved a little to make some space. Shanmugam extended his hands towards the flame and looked around at their faces. His head jerked involuntarily in sudden fear.

A sudden burst of incoherent babble came from one of the sleeping figures in the near distance. Perhaps if he knew Telugu he might have understood the prattle. As he continued to squat on his haunches, his legs began to ache. Since the cold had receded a little, he got up and began walking again.

He arrived at the bus terminus. It was deserted. A few lights were on in some of the rooms at the T.I.F.R. hostel premises on the opposite side.

He could not stand there indefinitely. He didn't feel like walking endlessly in the cold either. What was the time? It would be at least another hour before the raid concludes.

The veranda at the Post Office would be a haven against the cold. He considered sitting there for a while. The Devi Nagar Post Office was built like a small house in a village with a dwarf wall enclosing its veranda. He could sit with his back to the wall and stretch out. And perhaps even catch forty winks in that seated position.

It was only when he entered the post office that he appreciated the reality of the outside world. Barring the entrance, there were human beings prone everywhere around the compound, lying asleep like so many wrung-out dishrags. In the illumination provided by the streetlights he could see a few tin cans and walking sticks propped up near some of the sleeping figures. They were using cloth bundles as pillows.

Shanmugam leaned against the doorway to the post office and stretched out his legs. The very act felt relaxing.

As time went by, the cold began to bite. His bare feet jutting out of his trouser legs telegraphed the discomfort. He tucked his hands into his armpits for warmth, but his earlobes, face and lips bore the brunt. His nose breathed in the cold. He wouldn't last very long in this position. Several thoughts spiralled in his mind. The cold did not abate. One of the persons near him woke up, fumbled around and lit a beedi. In the flare of the match Shanmugam caught sight of the shiny stubs of the man's deformed fingers.

A feeling of revulsion swept over Shanmugam. He felt a prickling sensation all over his body. He got up swiftly and began walking aimlessly again. He walked briskly to overcome the cold. He turned left at the Afghan Church and walked towards Cuffe Parade. A slight feeling of warmth spread through his body and it felt pleasant. He walked past the bungalow whimsically named the 'Nook' and the clutch of skyscrapers emerging at the Backbay Reclamation. He stood at the northern end of the road.

He then turned around and began walking back towards Devi Nagar.

—

It had been three months since he was on the job. He had gone through five years' worth of purchase orders and compiled a comprehensive price list. He has also organised the files relating to the vendors – both alphabetically and by their products – after going through piles of papers that were lying around in disorganised heaps. He also managed to put in order invoice copies, challans relating to local vendors and outstation suppliers, incoming orders, quotations, Head Office correspondence, correspondence with customers and so on.

The factory has been in existence for several years now. But it did not appear as though anyone had taken the trouble or the initiative to keep things in order. Shanmugam felt that a little effort was all that was required to bring about some organisation. But it did not seem as though his efforts found much favour with Acharya.

Acharya was around twenty-one years of age. He was a Mangalorean. His speech still carried a child-like lisp. He was desperately trying to grow a moustache out of baby fuzz. His uncle occupied an important position at the company's Head Office. He had taken up his position here immediately after passing his Grade XI examination, thanks to his uncle's influence. Dikmani gave him a very long rope. As such, the supervisors and workmen all feared Acharya. To everyone around, other than Dikmani, his word was law.

Despite his youth, he was an extremely hard worker. And he had great memory power. He knew how to extract work out of others. He had a lot of responsibilities in view of his position. And yet, he acted childishly sometimes.

Shanmugam presented a threat to Acharya right from the beginning. First of all, he was a south Indian. Secondly, his educational qualifications trumped Acharya's. And, lastly, he was a sincere worker.

Acharya would respond only half-heartedly to Shanmugam's queries. He was careful to ensure Shanmugam did not learn more than what was absolutely necessary. He would only say 'transcribe this from that' but did not care to elaborate why. He kept certain jobs to himself. If you went near him at such times, he would shut down whatever he was doing and look up as if to ask 'what do you want?' The others did not seem to mind this behaviour. As far as they were concerned, they were only too happy not to be saddled with any additional work. For all that, it wasn't as if it was rocket science. Shanmugam had got the hang of it within the first two to three months of joining. Instead of sitting idly, he took on whatever was needed to be done. After all, posting Cardex, writing godown advices, updating pincards, keeping track of returns and local purchases were not complicated tasks. But every time Shanmugam did any of these of his own volition, he could discern hostility in Acharya's eyes. There were absolutely no traces of friendliness in them ever. It was also apparent that he made disparaging remarks about him whenever Shanmugam left his seat to either eat lunch or to empty his bladder.

He began to worry about how he would survive and continue to function in such a hostile environment.

The supply of bread was becoming erratic. Bakeries were not receiving their regular quota of flour from the ration shops. And bakeries found it more profitable to use the available flour to bake biscuits rather than bread.

Earlier, every shop in Devi Nagar used to stock bread in sufficient quantities. Both brands–Britannia and Modern– were readily available. Modern bread appeared better looking with neat, clean-cut slices. But, the taste of Britannia bread was far better. Shanmugam was in the habit of buying Britannia bread. Apart from these two popular brands, several local brands were also available. A small loaf would contain eleven slices. This was too much for one day, but not enough for two days. He would stretch a loaf for two days, eating six slices on the first and five on the second day.

Bananas with thick, green peels were available in plenty and he would buy half a dozen of them at a time to supplement his meals.

Bread, butter and jam became a boring breakfast choice after a while. He would wolf this combo down only when faced with dire hunger. Some days, Surve would offer him tea. He would then dunk his bread in it and have it for breakfast. Eating out at a restaurant was a distant pipedream. Sundar annan had left behind his stove and a supply of kerosene. He would occasionally boil an egg on it.

Every alternate day, the first thing he would do was buy a loaf of bread. For the last few days, there has been a bread famine. Shops were supplied bread in limited quantities. And they ran out as soon as they arrived. Queues began to form outside shops. Some mornings he had to wake up very early just to stand outside the shop. And the timing of the bread delivery was uncertain. He couldn't afford to stand outside the shop indefinitely. Even if he did, there was no guarantee that he would receive his quota of bread that day.

On the days he couldn't get bread, he would purchase the local equivalent called 'pav'. It would have a hard outer crust and a soft interior. He would buy two 'pavs', each with a set of four mini loaves. When he ate it, the crust would sometimes poke or even bruise the insides of his mouth.

Sundar annan was friendly with a shopkeeper to whom he would supply rice from his ration quota and rum at a subsidised rate. Taking advantage of that relationship, Shanmugam explained his predicament to the shopkeeper in his pidgin Hindi when no one was around at the store. The man asked Shanmugam to wait at the cross road to the garrison workshop every second day at 5.30 in the morning when he would supply him with a loaf of bread.

This practice continued for seven to eight days. As agreed, the shopkeeper would pedal past his location on a bicycle and fling a loaf of bread at him as he passed by. A sardarji saw Shanmugam collect his quota of bread in this manner one morning and turned up at the same spot the next day. Within a few days, a small crowd, with their pyjama cords dangling, began gathering at that spot in wait for the shopkeeper. The exasperated man finally began taking a different route to his shop thereafter.

If he went to work having had bread for breakfast, he would start feeling hungry again at around 11.00 o'clock. If he skipped breakfast altogether, hunger pangs would strike even earlier. At 1.00 in the afternoon the gurkha would ring the bell to signal lunch. For the first few days, Shanmugam ate the 'rice plate' on offer at a Mangalore Shetty eatery called 'Sujatha'. Six pooris, a bowl of rice, a bowl of dal, a bowl of sambar–the last two more clear water than gravy–a mixed vegetable curry made up of flat beans, white pumpkin or bottle gourd with black-eyed peas or gram and a piece of pickle. All this at a cost of one and a quarter rupees. Dal and sambar would be replenished on demand. Shanmugam's only aim was to fill his stomach with whatever was available and, therefore, he would lick his plate clean. If the waiter was a familiar figure, he would also ask for the vegetables in the sambar to be served to him. When he saw some of the others around him remove the vegetables from their sambar and keep them to one side before eating, he would feel heartsick. Some customers would bring their own large, thick chapatis from home, order either a plate of dal, sambar or usal with potato vada. They would tear and dip the chapatis into the gravy and consume them. A few ordered just a plate of usal and a couple of pavs which cost them only eight annas. When he came out of the eatery, Shanmugam would feel full. But that was a mere illusion. Around three in the afternoon, he would again start feeling hungry. More than the hunger, he hated the sour taste it produced in his mouth.

In one corner of the Atlas Mills Compound, two Malayali brothers from Cannanore–Abdul and Moosa–ran a canteen with the help of a few young boys. Their tea glasses smelt of onion. The plates reeked of eggs. At lunchtimes they would serve rice, dal, a potato and peas curry and omelette. Sometimes they would serve minced mutton as a special dish. It took some time for Shanmugam to realise that the 'mutton' was in reality beef and that's why they were able to provide it so cheaply. Once he learnt this, he stopped eating the mince.

If you ordered rice and dal, they would throw in a few slices of onion and two green chillies free of charge. When he grew tired of eating at the Shetty eatery, Shanmugam would buy rice, dal and curry from the Cannanore brothers. Some days he would forego the curry altogether. Night meals were a repeat of the same with no major variations.

Sometimes the rice would contain tiny stones. It would always have a few unhusked grains. An occasional strand of hair or a few maggots would not be unusual either. He would quietly remove these before eating. If the same thing had happened back home, he would have hurled the plate away and thrown a major temper tantrum. Here, he didn't dare point these out to the owners.

He had lost a lot more weight.

He now needed to fold his trousers twice to hold them up around his waist. His shirt appeared as though he had borrowed it from someone bigger than himself. His protruding shoulder bones and sunken cheeks evoked self-pity when he viewed himself in the mirror. Sometimes, on his way back from work in the evenings, he would falter as though from weakness. Every letter from home would advise him to take good care of himself. He just didn't know how he was supposed to do that.

There were some ten, fifteen days before Sundar annan would return from leave. If his family came along with him, he couldn't continue to stay on here. He needed to find another accommodation through Sundar annan's contacts. Food would continue to be a problem. There was no solution in sight for that particular issue. Matunga was said to be a bachelors' paradise. Good food, both lunch and dinner, would be available. Tamil movies were galore and so were silk saris. But, unfortunately, Shanmugam was in no position to frequent that paradise as often as he would have wished.

The search for alternative accommodation began. When Sundar annan came home, so did a bombshell ordering his transfer to Goa. He immediately became busy with his moving arrangements.

Rugs and blankets were washed and hung out to dry. The water drum was cleaned and repainted. All the miscellaneous utensils were stuffed into a large footlocker. All navy personnel owned a wooden trunk measuring four feet long, three feet wide and three feet high. On it would be written in paint 'G.M. Mathai, Jodhpur to Nasik', or something similar identifying the person and his itinerary. When he reached his destination, a folded rug would be placed on the box to turn it into a two-seater couch. Or a cot for an eight-year old child. As soon as the transfer order was received, into the footlocker would go the rolling board, rolling pin, stove, cooking vessels, miscellaneous utensils, coconut scraper, besom…Similarly, the water drum would acquire a lid and be stuffed with bedding items. Sack cloth would be sewn around it and it would be booked into the goods section of the train as oversized baggage. Quarters would have been either allotted at the new station or the family would have to share accommodation with someone belonging to their own community or an acquaintance introduced by a common friend. These arrangements would mostly be completed prior to the departure date.

Sundar annan took great care to ensure that all his effects reached the new station safely. His focus was also on securing comfortable quarters that was suitably furnished.

His ticket had been booked for Sunday. Another four or five days left. This meant three days of home-cooked food. Forgotten tastes and smells. To Shanmugam, who had concluded that anything other than bread was a delicacy, each meal seemed to be a feast.

His search for living arrangements was proving complicated. But there was no option but to move out. Sundar annan suggested that he speak to a few people at Devi Nagar to see if Shanmugam could perhaps stay on for another month or so. But the checking parties posed a huge problem. Many Malayalis continued to stay on as 'illegals' for years together. But Shanmugam felt he lacked the confidence to pull off such a feat.

When he learnt that there was accommodation available in Meadows Street at the Fort area near Flora Fountain,

Shanmugam went there to check it out along with Sundar annan at around 8.30 one night. It was on the third floor of Ketan Chambers. It was not a residence, but an office. Since business hours were over, tables, chairs, cupboards, files and cabinets seemed prominent in the deserted workplace.

Three UP bhaiyas were busy preparing their evening meal. One was kneading dough for chapatties. Dal was cooking on a Primus stove. Another was busily chopping onions and potatoes. Tomatoes, cilantro, chillies and garlic were kept ready on a nearby plate. It was pitch dark outside. Footsteps could be heard scurrying on the wooden staircase outside.

It seemed that these three men were employed as peons in that office and lived on the premises. If Shanmugam were to share their accommodation, no one should be made aware of his presence. He should be gone before nine every morning and should not return before eight at night. He was allowed to stay in only on Sundays. There were common bath and toilet facilities for the whole floor. He should keep his trunk and bed hidden behind a cupboard. He shouldn't hang any clothes outside. What about a wet towel? Bathing was to be done only in the evenings. Clothes should be washed only on Saturday evenings.

The place seemed clean enough. The location was also very convenient and at the centre of the city. But, what was he to do on Saturday afternoons and on those days when his day-offs overlapped with the firm's working days? And where was he to go if he came down with a headache or fever and wanted to simply lie down and take it easy?

Subbiah, who was employed at the dockyard, suggested that he look for accommodation in a chawl at Dharavi. So, on Wednesday evening he caught a train from Reay Road and alighted at Mahim Station. He could see a number of Tamilians around. He asked one of them directions to Ramarwadi. The man offered to take Shanmugam there.

"Where are you from, anne?"

"Kalakkad."

"Are you staying at Ramarwadi too?"

"Yes…who're you visiting there?"

"Subbiah who works at the dockyard…"

"Which Subbiah? The one from Ervadi? But he stays at the Muthuramalingam chawl, doesn't he? How do you know him?"

"He's an acquaintance of one of my fellow-villagers. I need to see him about accommodation."

"Do you belong to the Thevar community?"

"No…"

"Then how can you stay at the Muthuramalingam chawl? That's meant only for the Thevars. Anyway, go and meet Subbiah. He probably has some plan in mind."

Sewage flowed all along the path. There were heaps of garbage lying all around. The road was extremely congested. A mountainous pile of broken glass bottles lay heaped in front of a shop. Crumpled and torn bundles of paper were stacked in a mammoth pile inside another shop. Old and dirty polythene sheets were piled in a jumbo hoard inside a third.

All along the route were food carts—sizzling woks frying samosas and fritters, full mackerels sautéed with their heads intact.

The neighbourhood was interspersed with Tamil signboards:

'Gajalakshmi Tiffin Stall'

'Arignar Anna Laundry'

'Kalaignar Hairdressers'

'Jeeva Printers'

'Periyar Tailors'

A plethora of party flags were in display. Newspapers highlighting MGR's challenge to Karunanidhi or Kalaignar's rousing speech at Madurai were flying off the shelves, depending upon the reader's party affiliation.

Unlike in other parts of Bombay, the men here appeared darker and thinner. Many wore shorts. All spoke loudly. Shanmugam asked the man accompanying him,

"Where do you work, annachi?"

"Pannalal Silk Mills…on Reay Road."

"Is your family here with you?"

"No. They're all back home. I stay here at a chawl."

"When did you visit home last?"

"It's been two years now. I'm planning to go again this year when I receive my Diwali bonus."

The air was thick with dust and flies. A group of children, wearing crumpled white shirts and khaki shorts, passed by.

"Do you have children, annachi?"

"The eldest boy is in the tenth class. The second girl has just now attained puberty, the youngest boy is in class four."

They reached Ramarwadi. A few persons were unloading wet, salted hides from a lorry. The smell was gut-wrenching, but people continued to walk by seemingly unaffected.

Subbiah was home and accompanied him to the next chawl.

It was a long building. There were fifteen rooms in a row on the ground floor and fifteen on the first. A central staircase serviced the building and gave access to a long passage which ran through the length of each floor. The passage was open on one side and had a row of doors on the other side, each door being the entrance to a room.

Subbiah took him into a long room, around twenty-five feet long and ten feet wide. At one end of the room was the bath area. Three large sixty-gallon drums stood there along with two or three plastic buckets and mugs.

Wooden planks, about fifteen to eighteen inches in width, were affixed to the room's walls. On one side of this makeshift shelf stood a line of old trunk boxes. A clothesline had been put up underneath the shelf on which were hung some twenty to twenty-five towels of various descriptions. The shelf on the other side was crammed with stoves, kerosene tins, aluminium utensils, rolling boards, plates and glasses.

Subbiah explained, "There's room for one more person. The rent is twenty rupees payable in advance. There are already twenty-seven people staying here. Some leave for work in the mornings and return in the evenings; some go to work in the afternoon and return the next morning. Some work the night shifts and sleep the whole day. Water is available only in the mornings and evenings. You need to store it during those times. Clothes should be washed when water supply is available. Toilet facilities are outside. If you go there at five in the morning, there wouldn't be too much of a crowd. It becomes busy thereafter till around eight o' clock. Chaps spend half an hour at a time inside, straining and pushing while smoking. There is no rush hour in the morning and so you can take a bath in the wash area."

All this seemed tolerable to him. So, Shanmugam said he'd be back on Sunday with his belongings and took his leave.

# 6

Sundar annan was scheduled to leave at 8.30 on Sunday morning by the Miraj Express. The final night passed sleeplessly. All their personal effects–barring those already booked on the train's freight van–were crammed into every available suitcase and trunk. The whole house was thoroughly inspected repeatedly to see if any item had been left behind. At 7.00 a.m., after a breakfast of bread and jam, Sundar annan went to fetch a military truck to transport them all to the railway station.

Shanmugam also packed his own personal belongings. Apart from the trunk he had brought with him from the village, he also bundled up his bedspread, pillow and a few old books. He then gathered up the few things that Sundar annan was leaving behind for his use: an old plastic bucket, aluminium mug, aluminium plate, aluminium tumbler, aluminium spoon, a butter knife, half a bottle of jam, some butter gathered up in a Horlicks bottle, a bottle of warmed-over coconut oil for his hair.

By the time Sundar annan came back with the truck, loaded all their stuff onto it and they arrived at V.T. station, it was

7.45. The Miraj Express stood ready on Platform No. 13. They unloaded the truck and stowed the luggage into the military compartment without the help of porters, though it took them three trips to complete the whole operation.

The train wasn't very crowded. They got a compartment with six seats for themselves. As there was still some time before the train departed, Sundar annan plied him with advice–as though he was a newlywed girl leaving her maternal home for the first time.

As time went by with Sundar annan bombarding him with his wisdom, Shanmugam felt a feverish warmth spread all over his body and mind. Tears welled up in his eyes. Sundaram patted his shoulders reassuringly and got on to the train. Shanmugam stood there for a while listlessly waving at the departing train.

It suddenly struck him that he was now all alone in a city of seven million people. There was no one he could turn to for support or assistance. He walked out holding the trunk in one hand, the plastic bucket in the other with the bedding tucked under his arm. A Harbour Line train stood on Platform No. 1 scheduled to depart for Bandra at 8.52.

It was ten in the morning when he reached Ramarwadi following the directions he had made a mental note of during his previous visit. Subbiah was at the chawl. He handed over the advance of twenty rupees. Subbiah then called out to one of the residents and announced loudly enough for everyone to hear that Shanmugam was now a new resident of that kholi.

In the wash area, one man was soaping himself all over while another was taking a bath, pouring mug after mug of water over himself. As one occupant returned from the toilet and put down an empty 2 kilo tin of 'Postman' oil, another picked it up, filled it with water and carrying a cigarette and matchbox, thrust his feet into a pair of plastic slippers and walked out towards the toilets. Another person was busy mixing washing powder and water in a bucket, raising a mountain of suds into which he dunked a pile of dirty clothes. One man sat cross-legged on the floor carefully shaving his face with the aid of a small mirror propped up on his trunk. Two persons were still asleep covered from head to toe in their blankets. One man was immersed in the latest issue of the Kumudam while another was perusing yesterday's Murasoli. Two persons were hurriedly getting dressed, anxious not to be late for an MGR movie. Six stoves were hissing with the sounds of food being prepared, while eight men were busy playing cards.

Shanmugam had no pressing engagements. He had also already performed his morning's ablutions. He had no one to visit either. He was not in the mood for a film. There was time enough to go out for lunch. He changed into a lungi and sat down. He thought he would write home. He had a stock of inland letter forms with him. He pulled his trunk towards him and, using it as a desk, began composing a letter.

—

It soon became apparent that eating out would be a problem. Even though the food and snacks were plentiful and to his taste–the servings were generously ladled out of buckets instead of being served in small bowls–the cleanliness and hygiene of the place was a major concern.

The floors were constantly wet. The greasy, wooden benches gave off a funky smell made up of years of spittle and spilt water. Flies buzzed around, tin tumblers were coated with an oily film and, if you happened to glance into the kitchen area from the wash-up zone, it resembled a filthy cattle shed.

Sometimes, while passing stools, his rectum would experience a burning sensation. He often heard murmurs and grumblings from his stomach which sometimes also smarted badly. In a few days he developed severe diarrhoea.

He began passing thin, watery stools. He needed to visit the toilet more frequently than usual. Unfortunately, the arrangements at the chawl did not provide him with the facility to visit the toilet as often as he needed to. The office did not fare better in this aspect either. The factory compound boasted six communal toilets none of which was fitted with doors. The factory workers would defecate with one finger stretched out to warn others that the premises were occupied. The toilet bowls were forever brimming with excrement and reeking with a foul stink.

His roommates generously offered suggestions for home remedies.

Eat a banana mashed up with pori and split gram.

Eat 250 grams of halwah in two sittings. Squeeze a lemon into a glass of milk and drink it up. Brew some tea and drink it with lemon juice without milk or sugar.

Liquefy a whole pomegranate, peel and all, and drink up the concoction.

None of these cures worked. His ailment continued. Then somebody suggested that he take Chlorostrep, a tablet costing eight rupees-odd for a strip of ten, for over four days. This is what finally helped. He made a note of its name for future use. For several days he had subsisted on rice and yogurt only. It was not as though rice and yogurt came cheap at Bombay eateries. It seemed the runs were a common 'boon' to many Bombay bachelors. There were two other blessings in addition: jaundice and chicken pox. If you lived there for seven to eight years at a stretch, you were sure to catch one, two or even all three of these diseases. There seemed to be no immediate escape from their clutches either. If you frequented a slightly more hygienic restaurant, you may gain some relief.

There were two messes in Matunga. They apparently charged one hundred and twenty rupees a month for two meals a day.

You had to enrol yourself and pay the full amount in advance. You also had to hand over your ration card so they could purchase rice with it.

Two things deterred Shanmugam. First, he couldn't afford to spend two rupees for each meal. Secondly, he needed to be at work by 9.00 o'clock whereas these eateries didn't start serving food until then.

However, the food at these places tended to be hygienic, tasty and plentiful. He had eaten there on one or two occasions, when he was flush with cash fresh from receiving his salary. A meal had cost him two and a half rupees. Two curries, sambar, rasam, buttermilk, papadum with plenty of rice, and even a spoonful of ghee. But the tempo of the place unnerved him. He had to constantly look in the direction from where the items were being brought in by the servers and shovel his food in, like one would at wedding feasts in his village. Also, the custom of people standing behind him, breathing down his neck, waiting for him to finish and vacate the spot, irritated him to no end.

Another important factor was that both these messes were run by Brahmins. Even though no overt form of untouchability was evident in Bombay, at certain points in time he could not help but feel like an 'outsider' at these places. Facial features, accent and the manner of eating tended to distinguish a Brahmin from 'the others'. Since nearly 98% of the members at these messes tended to be Brahmins, they enjoyed special privileges—or, at least, so it seemed to Shanmugam. That entitlement felt exclusionary to him.

Within a month, Shanmugam had eaten at several different places for a change, to try out new flavours, or because it suited his budget.

He was told that another Malayali mess was operating at King's Circle, on the second floor of the Murugan Stores building.

After returning from work, he had a wash, got dressed again and set out after seven thirty to try out the new place.

Food was served on banana leaves spread on the floor. Unlimited quantities of Kerala rice accompanied by sambar, rasam along with fish curry and pickles. Shanmugam had learnt from bitter experience not to ask for yogurt or buttermilk at Malayali restaurants. You couldn't stand their rancid smell and sour taste. The cost of this meal was one rupee and thirty paise. If you wanted fried fish, mutton, egg curry or yogurt, that cost extra. Another lesson that Shanmugam had learnt was not to order any mutton dishes at Malayali eateries. For they seemed to hold the European point of view that beef was far superior in taste compared to goat's meat.

Shanmugam felt that the food was not too bad as it reminded him of the meals he had eaten at the messes back home in the village.

The eatery consisted of just one room. Three brothers cooked in the same hall and served the customers. The hand-wash area and the bin used for dumping the used banana leaves were a bit messy but not majorly off-putting. Generally speaking, Malayalis were sticklers for cleanliness. After he had had one or two meals there, he found out that he could broker a monthly tab with them. Shanmugam made some further enquiries and discovered that he had to pay one hundred rupees in advance and settle the account by the tenth of each following month.

On an average, there would be thirty dinners a month. Plus lunch on five Sundays. Even if he ordered an additional dish occasionally, it would not exceed fifty rupees a month. This seemed workable. But the advance payment of a hundred rupees posed a major hurdle. Which expense was he supposed to curtail to produce this amount? With much heartache he reckoned he could perhaps stop the remittance of fifty rupees back home. But what about the remainder?

He ate at that place continuously for several days. On occasions he was forced to return to the chawl from the office, have a wash and put on the same clothes again to go to the mess for his dinner. He found he couldn't bear his hunger on such days. Though dinner was scheduled for 7.00 p.m., they began serving it as early as 6.45. So he began to catch a train from his office, get down at King's Circle station, hang around the area for a while and go in for his dinner. On some days the food would be ready. On others, rice would still be cooking. He would then wait for a while for the food to be made ready.

He would take the opportunity to strike up a conversation with the brothers running the mess. The 'uncle' cooking rice would ask about him. It was an advantage arriving there early for his dinner. One could avoid the wet slickness on the ground where the banana leaves would be laid, the litter at the hand-wash area and where the used leaves were dumped, and the all-pervading, mildly sour smell of cooking.

He then gathered up courage to ask one of the brothers, "I can only afford to pay an advance of fifty rupees. Will you let me enrol as a member?" and felt massively relieved when the man nodded his assent.

After dinner, if he caught a train from King's Circle to Mahim and walked back to the chawl, he would be there between 7.45 and 8.00 p.m. But the place would be abuzz with activity at that time of the night. The clamorous sound of cooking would make it impossible to sit quietly and catch one's breath. He wouldn't be able to make his bed and lie down before 10 o' clock at night. So he began spending some time pottering around the city before returning home.

There would be some cement benches facing the road at Maheshwari Udyan. One could sit there and watch the world go by.

On the park's lawns there would be frequent gatherings of associations and trade unions that did not have their own place for such meetings. Or else, there would be some six or seven elders, bespectacled retired men with false teeth and rheumy eyes holding walking sticks, chatting among themselves. He would listen in on them with an air of insouciance.

If he couldn't snag a bench all to himself, he would share a seat with others. There would be a cross-section of ages among those occupying the park benches. Most of them appeared defeated, bitter and full of self-loathing.

The families and friends who occupied the lawns and those who sat on the benches seemed to be on two entirely different wavelengths. Some days even this activity would pall. Perhaps he wouldn't experience these thoughts and feelings of loneliness and hatred if only he had a few friends.

Everyone at the factory was familiar, but not friendly. It was the same case at the chawl as well. How long was he to continue like this? The park attendant blew his whistle. It was 9 o'clock. He would not be permitted to sit there any longer and build his castles in the air. The curfew was in place to prevent anti-social activities. But it was well known that certain shenanigans did take place in the park after closing time with the connivance of the caretaker.

—

It was Kathamuthu whose bed was adjacent to his. He suggested that Shanmugam should get a stove and a few utensils and start cooking for himself. Or else, he could join a group that cooked their own food.

Shanmugam recalled his observations during the course of his stay there: Fire up the stove, place on it a vessel containing water, clean the rice off stones, grain and other impurities, wash it and add it to the water, it would start boiling; while the rice cooked, peel potatoes, chop onions, slice green chillies and prepare a mixture of tamarind and water. When the rice was done, remove it from the stove, place a wok in its place, sauté some mustard seeds in oil, add coriander seeds, turmeric and chilli powder; cook for a while; add the onions and the tamarind mixture, and when the whole thing comes to a boil, add the potatoes and cook till it is done. This gravy would do for dinner and the next morning's meal. For accompaniment, he could prepare a dry curry of either cabbage or beans without the addition of coconut. Or, on occasions, he could just prepare rice and buy either sambar or fish curry from the eatery opposite for eight annas.

However, this would take up all his evenings and nights. In addition, there was also the chore of dishwashing. All in all, Shanmugam did not feel this would be feasible.

He had started to develop a sense of friendship with Kathamuthu over the last few days.

Kathamuthu was two or three years younger than Shanmugam. He was employed in the departmental canteen at V.T station. He had earlier worked at four or five eateries and had secured this position through the recommendation of Melapanaiyur Muthusamy annachi. Given this background, it went without saying that his salary was really not worth writing home about. But he received free rail passes for travel to and from his hometown. Kathamuthu managed to enjoy much prestige back home among his relatives and townsfolk by splurging a cool thousand rupees every time he went home on leave, and by falsely claiming to be employed with Central Railways.

Whenever Kathamuthu returned to the chawl after a late-night movie or having worked the second shift, everyone else at the tenement would be prone on the floor fast asleep. If anyone was absent, his space, approximately two feet wide, would be vacant. Whenever Kathamuthu was late coming back, Shanmugam would spread his bed out in his allotted space.

A dim light would be burning. In a little while, someone would put it out also. Like moss slowly creeping over the surface of a pond, the occupants of the kholi would move about in their sleep and position themselves throughout the night so as to cover every available inch of space in the room. A latecomer would face several problems. If he switched on a light, there would be hisses of disapproval from all corners of the room. Relying on his night vision, he would have to tiptoe through the mass of bodies lying on the floor and find his assigned spot with the help of the familiar odour of his towel hanging on the line above it.

Shift a bit…

Upon hearing the voice, bodies would inch about a bit and the latecomer would have to insert himself between the heaving masses and lie down amongst them. He would then have to move his neighbours' hands or legs that might accidentally fall on him during the course of sleep.

If you are woken up by the bustle created by the first-shifters, who switch on the light and cause quite a flutter, you will find each of the men sleeping in a signature pose: with hands between thighs, drooling, snoring on his back, lying on his stomach, hunched up on all fours like a frog, mouth wide open, oblivious to his disheveled dhoti revealing his morning wood.

Kathamuthu would receive letters every week without fail. All the chawl-dwellers used the address of the laundry on the main road at the turn-off, worried that letters addressed to them at the chawl might get misdelivered.

His letters would be addressed to:

S. K. Muthu,
C/o. Arignar Anna Laundry,
Kumbharwada Road,
Dharavi,
Bombay 400017.

Normally, when returning home from work, he would stop at the laundry and go through the stack of mail to see if any letter addressed to him had arrived. If Kathamuthu was working the late shift, Shanmugam would collect his letters for him.

"Here, read this, annachi," he would extend a letter to Shanmugam. If it was from his uncle at Aralvaimozhi, it would be on the following lines: look after yourself, avoid roaming around in the sun, send money regularly to your amma, reply soon. If it was from Esanthimangalam, it would read 'this is your sister writing on amma's dictation, there have been no rains here this monsoon, the crops need to be transplanted, the Pechi corner of the field is overrun with weeds, send an extra fifty rupees this month, Shanmugavelu thatha from the South Street passed away four days ago, we are all fine here, drink milk every night before going to bed'.

Even though only four such letters would arrive each month, since their arrival dates varied, he would visit the laundry every day. As soon as he went and stood in front of the shop, the laundry-owner, Madasamy, would drop a bundle of letters before him which he would rummage through. The letters in the bundle would range from ones that were three-months-old to those that had arrived just yesterday, crumpled, dog-eared and forlorn.

That evening, when he got off at Mahim and was walking to the chawl, Shanmugam heard someone hailing him from behind. He turned back to see Kathamuthu walking fast to catch up with him. He slowed down his own pace till Kathamuthu neared him.

The evening sun lent its colour to the rising dust particles. A poster hung on a red-coloured staff. It seemed that a Comrade was scheduled to address a meeting that Friday.

At an adjoining shop, Kathamuthu bought a copy of Kutheeti, a Communist publication. He was a supporter of that party. It carried extracts of the speech by their leader at the Tamukkam Ground in Madurai three days ago.

"Annachi, let's have a cup of tea," Muthu suggested. They had tea and vadai while leafing through the periodical.

At the laundry, Muthu leafed through the bundle of letters. There was an envelope addressed to him. It was obviously from his uncle at Aralvaimozhi. Only he would address his communications with his nephew's full name, 'Kathamuthu'. But he was normally in the habit of sending postcards only unless he had gone on a pilgrimage to the Sudalaimadan temple and offered prayers and offerings there, or to the Chithoor Thenkarai Maharaja temple, when he would send sacred ash as devotional offerings from these sites in an envelope. But that would only be during the auspicious months of Masi and Panguni, never in Aippasi. Muthu therefore carefully folded the letter and put it in his pocket presuming that the letter contained some matter of import. It was not possible for him to open it up and read the letter then and there. Since he needed to spell out the letters and his uncle's handwriting was not the most legible in the world, he needed to take his time.

It was past seven when they reached the chawl. The place was frantic with several groups busy cooking — the roaring hiss of some seven or eight stoves, the kneading of dough for chapattis, the removal of impurities from rice, the chopping of vegetables, the aroma of sambar cooking on a few stoves, a man crushing coconut and spices on a grindstone...

"Ramaswamy, let me have an onion."

"I don't have any. Why don't you get your own?"

"All right, all right. I'll replace it tomorrow. Let me have one now."

There were many such instances of territorial usurpations.

Kumaraswamy went out with a Horlicks bottle. Since he had run out of vegetables and spices, he was presumably going to get either sambar or fish curry from the nearby shop.

Shanmugam changed into a lungi and sat on the bench outside. Kathamuthu followed him shortly thereafter with the letter in his hand. It seemed Muthu wasn't in the mood to cook that evening. In the mornings, he would have his breakfast at the canteen. Lunch was also taken care of there. He would cook at night whenever he felt like it. In this matter, he had earned the envy of many. "Lucky fellow! He manages to save his entire salary."

Muthu got up from the bench, lit a beedi from the flame of one of the burning stoves, took two or three deep drags on it and extracted the letter from the cover. There were a total of three pages.

"That's quite thick! Is it a love letter?"

"Oh shut up. It's from my uncle."

He began to read, spelling out each letter. As he went on reading laboriously, his face reflected happiness initially, then worry and irritation.

His heart melted when he thought of his uncle's daughter. Since he was his maternal uncle, it was customary for Muthu to spend a couple of days at Panakkudi every time he went home on leave. The place was quite a change from the paddy-growing Nanjil Nadu region to which he belonged. Just walking with the reddish soil of the land coating his feet would make his heart soar. Banana groves, maize, rye, chillies, thorny acacia trees lined up near ponds, ochre-coloured pools of water, stepwells with bullocks raising the water from them, and, around the wells, okra, aubergines, broad beans, pigeon peas...

He had totally fallen in love with her when he had visited them last year during his holidays. One evening when no one was around, he was seated on a bench pretending grandly to read a weekly when she placed a slightly unripe guava next to him, ran into the house and stood there laughing.

Kathamuthu sat with his head lowered for a while.

Accommodation was going to be a huge problem.

He couldn't stay at the chawl with his wife. His uncle had already fixed the date for the wedding. Then there were transport expenses, dresses, jewellery…

He gave the letter to Shanmugam and asked him to keep the news to himself for the time being. While they went out to eat, he kept on talking. He couldn't say no to his uncle. His family wouldn't back him if he demurred. There was no way out.

The loan he had taken to meet the expenses for last year's trip home had just been paid off. If he wanted to rent half a room at the neighbouring chawl, he needed to pay up two thousand rupees in advance.

On being questioned about his uncle's daughter, Muthu squirmed with shyness. He asked Shanmugam to wait next to the Dakshinamara Nadar Sangam and went to meet the chit fund operator from Vadakkankulam.

When he returned, his face appeared a lot brighter.

# 7

Nothing exciting was happening at work.

Acharya was still intent on keeping Shanmugam at bay. He was not very worried about the others. Perhaps that's why he never took even a day off. He was also the first to arrive and the last to leave the workplace. Shanmugam had never seen him arrive late for work. It's been three years since Acharya had last visited his hometown. He had accumulated leave totalling sixty-three days to his credit. If he ever went on a holiday, he would take two months off at a stretch. Someone else would then have to officiate on his behalf during those two months. Perhaps Acharya feared that the substitute might overthrow him in his absence.

If Acharya was not around, who amongst those present would perform his duties?

Sathyavan Shivaram Raut's only previous experience was applying spindle oil to spinning machines.

Shivaji 'Chandu' Dele was quite an intelligent person. But all his intelligence seemed focussed on exploring and discovering the best red light areas in Bombay – Faras Road, Falkland

Road, Jamuna Mansion, Hanuman Galli, and so on – all of which he patronised regularly. Throughout the day, he would be busy describing his sexploits with the women he had bedded the previous night. He would declare that the 'Nepali chokri' was A-1 or the 'Madrassi maal' was first-class. He would also proudly boast that the large quantities of country liquor he had consumed the night before had had little or no impact on his sexual performance. He would also be generous with tips regarding the winning numbers for the daily Kalyan matka lottery. Like royals and party leaders were bestowed appellations by fawning courtiers and hangers-on, he liberally conferred on everyone the choicest of epithets—'motherfucker', 'bastard', 'arsehole' and so on. And if this was not enough, he was also in the habit of constantly demanding a 'small loan', ranging from three to five rupees, from anyone who crossed his path. He somehow never seemed to have sufficient hours left in a day after attending to his Kalyan matka and other gambling activities.

Aaron Reuben Penkar was a Dutch Jew who had taken up employment here after retiring from the Port Trust. He was waiting for an El Al aircraft to arrive from Israel to ferry him to the Promised Land. His daughter was the Personal Assistant to the Chief Executive at the Head Office, which explained why he was employed here on a contract basis in his sixty-sixth year. You couldn't help but feel somewhat sorry when you saw him napping at his desk behind his thick glasses.

Shyam Charan Shukla was quite a clever man. But he was more interested in roaming around all day in the name of 'local purchases' while lining his own pockets in the process.

The fact that each one of them was busily engaged in his own affairs worked to Acharya's advantage. And, in turn, it suited them that he assumed all the responsibilities at the workplace. Shanmugam's presence was thus an irritant to him, like encountering sand grains in a mouthful of spinach. On the whole, Acharya deserved his position at work due to his diligence and intelligence. He also belonged to a well-to-do family. His sister lived in an 800 square feet flat in Sion which consisted of three rooms and a kitchen. His brother-in-law was in the areca nut business. They even had a telephone at home. Shanmugam had often noticed Acharya asking certain parties to call him at home after 7.00 p.m. He also generously advanced loans of fifty and a hundred rupees to the workmen at the factory.

At lunchtime, Acharya would receive a lunch box from home. He would unlock the metal carrier and pull out a tiffin box. Shanmugam would be seated at his desk, eating his rice and dal from Moosa's stall. Dish after dish would scent the air. Salivating, he would sneak an envious peek at the spread. Apart from the regular dishes, there would always be a sweet – burfi, halwa or peda. There would also be some fruit: an apple, an orange, a couple of bananas, sliced mangoes or a bunch of grapes. A salad consisting of sliced cucumber, tomatoes and carrot would also be on the menu.

Initially, for a couple of days, either for formality's sake or out of genuine hospitality, Acharya invited Shanmugam to share his meal. Realising that he had nothing to offer in return to an Udupi Brahmin named Acharya, Shanmugam refused politely. The invitations were never renewed thereafter. As he picked out grain and worm castings from his rice, Shanmugam pretended not to notice Acharya smirking with either disdain or revulsion. For he knew very well he would never get an opportunity to retaliate in the same fashion.

Despite eating well, Acharya possessed a thin, lanky frame. He resembled a long string bean. While his height was nearly six feet, his weight wouldn't have been more than forty-three kilos. His main grouse was that the fuzz on his face did not metamorphose to a proper moustache. His face was still covered with pimples.

He also had at his fingertips the names, catalogue numbers and inventory numbers of over a thousand spare parts for all their machines. Shanmugam, on the other hand, did not know the difference between a bolt, a stud and a screw. Neither did he know that screws came in different shapes – hexagonal, flat, domed, Phillips, star – nor heard of things like grub screws, socket sets or knurling. Whereas, Acharya, as soon as he looked at a spare, would rattle off its catalogue number, '44-338-7C2'. He probably even knew the material, size and whether its threading was UNF, BSF or BSW. Shanmugam was in awe of such proficiency in a man who was only twenty-one years of age and had just three years' experience. The only deficiency, if you could call it that, was a certain weakness in Acharya's spoken and written English. But, to the management who were content that the work at the factory was running smoothly, this did not represent a major shortcoming.

Acharya also enjoyed a lot of privileges and concessions with the Works Manager, Dikmani. He often hitched rides in Dikmani's car after work. If Dikmani was delayed, Acharya would call him up on the telephone. Where Shanmugam was paid two hundred and ten rupees, Acharya's salary was six hundred and fifty rupees.

There were two telephones at the workplace on the Manager's desk. Acharya had been provided with extensions to both, with calling and trunk dialling facilities.

There would be plenty of calls every day. Acharya wouldn't allow anyone else to answer the phones. If he was in the toilet or in the assembly line when it rang, he would come running back to his desk. None of the other employees would even bother to pick up the telephone in his absence. Shanmugam would sometimes summon up his courage and answer a call saying 'Hello, Thompsons'. By then Acharya would come rushing back and signal him frantically to hand over the receiver to him. If, in order to wind him up, Shanmugam asked some question of the caller just to delay the handover, Acharya would impatiently start hopping from foot to foot, and appear ready to snatch the telephone from his hand.

Shanmugam felt that Dikmani, despite his serious exterior, was a good person. Therefore, when he was not very busy, and when Acharya was inside the workshop, he gathered up courage and went into Dikmani's office. Generally, there was no interaction between the Manager and the staff. As he entered the cool air-conditioned office, Dikmani raised his head and looked at him. The temperature inside the cabin appeared to drop further. He said, "Excuse me sir, I need to speak to you. I have a lot of spare time after completing my normal daily duties, and I'd like to learn more about the workings of the factory if that can be arranged." Dikmani said that he would look into it.

No one knows what he told Acharya, but the next day a file full of bills and a bunch of godown advices landed on Shanmugam's desk. He was to match them by category, catalogue number, order number, amount and cross reference each, note them down in a register, obtain the Manager's signature and send it to Head Office by recorded delivery.

This kept him busy for a while. Earlier, the bills and the godown advices used to be sent out separately and at random. There was no correlation between the two thereafter.

At the end of the month, he consulted the ledger and prepared a report. They had bought spares worth Rs. 639,760.80 during the month of March. When he compared that figure with purchases made in a few other months, it gave him a pleasant thrill to discover that a particular month's figures were lower by Rs. 60,000 and another's was higher by Rs. 35,000.

One day, a doubt suddenly popped up in Shanmugam. When they procured their material from Ahmedabad, they paid clearance charges of 2% while octroi duty, packing & forwarding charges and other miscellaneous charges totalled another 3%. Sometimes the rejection rate among the materials amounted to 10 to 20%. Why not debit the suppliers with these charges? He raised this question with Dikmani the next day. He said he'd consult with Head Office and revert. When he received Dikmani's go ahead the very next day, he began debiting the suppliers with these expenses. Initially, Acharya did not pay much heed to this revised practice. He pretended it was no big deal.

In addition, they were making cash purchases worth around thirty thousand rupees each month from one or two regular suppliers. The easy familiarity that Acharya displayed with them seemed to suggest that all was not above-board. As some petty cash bills passed through his hands in course of his duties, he became generally familiar with their pricing levels. The firm would benefit if most of these purchases were sourced directly from their original manufacturers. The price differential would be substantial. The quality of the products would be assured and they would also get a credit period of thirty to sixty days to make their payments.

He casually mentioned this to Dikmani one day. He immediately summoned Acharya who glared at him angrily. He tried to put up objections, stating that the delivery would be delayed, their responses would be irregular, they wouldn't be interested in small orders and so on. Dikmani instructed him to write to them enquiring about their prices.

Shanmugam had never drafted official letters before. He wanted to best display his knowledge and proficiency in English through these communications. The reference number came first. To indicate that the matter pertained to the Assembly Division, he started off with the letters AD with a stroke after it. He included his own initials RS and inserted another stroke. Then came the serial number and date. It took him nearly two hours to complete the first draft after several changes and corrections. He drafted six such letters and sent them off to be typed. Nothing happened for four days. Perhaps Acharya had intervened. He then typed them out himself using the hunt-and-peck method, checked them for errors and sent them to Dikmani for signature. Replies started coming in within ten days. He felt extremely proud when Dikmani marked them in red ink for his attention and passed them on to him.

The cash purchase that month reduced by twelve thousand. The regular suppliers came, circled around and went back disappointed. Shanmugam felt a sense of pleasure in their disappointment. He felt that, with a little more effort, a further eight to ten thousand rupees could be saved.

Acharya now turned into a sworn enemy.

—

Reuben Joseph was an assistant fitter employed in the factory's assembly line. Unlike Shanmugam, he spoke fluent English as he had studied in an English medium school. But he had quit studies after failing his Grade X exams. It was nice to chat with him, even if it was only for a few minutes, given that Shanmugam could not build a rapport with the others. Reuben said his family originally hailed from Washermanpet in Madras and that his father had come to Bombay when still a child and that he himself had never been to Tamil Nadu. Since some Tamil words were still in use at his house, he spoke a few colloquial Tamil words with an Anglo-Indian accent. Whenever they met in the mornings, he would greet Shanmugam with a sthothiram. Something of a camaraderie developed between the two of them.

During working hours, if he happened to come by to the store area – to answer a phone call, to wash his hands, to get some cotton waste or change damaged spares – Reuben would stop for a chat with Shanmugam.

"What are you up to today?"

"Have you heard from home?"

Acharya would watch this interaction out of the corner of his eye with irritation. Sometimes he would let out a loud 'tch' to express his disapproval. Or he would say "Kya hai Reuben?" in an admonitory tone. Reuben would stand his ground for a few moments ignoring the implied reprimand. He would then go back to his place and return carrying a screw with a faulty thread in his hand. His face would reflect satisfaction at having managed to ruffle Acharya's feathers.

Jacob, Reuben's father, had been a foreman in another division of that company. In that capacity, he had provided the initial training to many in the firm. A heavy drinker, he had dropped dead in the assembly line one afternoon.

The company immediately provided a job to Reuben. The other staff members had a soft corner for him.

He was a good worker but unpredictable. While returning from lunch break, he would bring with him a stray kitten and feed it a saucer of milk. He would target the unripe mangoes on the tree growing in the next compound.

He was slightly more educated than the other workers and carried himself well. As a result, despite his age – which was around 25 – he had assumed the role of a leader.

He was responsible for a water cooler being installed and tea being served, albeit at a cost, at the factory. His other demands included uniforms for workers, a hundred rupees raise for all.

Generally, after lunch, Shanmugam would go back to his seat and read something. Or he would go inside and watch a card game in progress there. Penkar never had lunch at the factory. After breakfast in the morning he would wait till he returned home to have his dinner. During lunch break he would go out, smoke a cigarette and have a paan. Occasionally, he would purchase a couple of bananas.

Whenever Shanmugam went to have lunch at Sujatha, on his way back, he would join Penkar who would be standing and watching the world go by at the entrance of the Atlas Mills compound. His favourite topic of conversation was Israel and he would wax eloquent on that subject. He said he was planning to retire within a few more years and migrate to Israel. All his relatives had gone there already one after another. He claimed he would receive retirement benefits there as he was past 60.

Reay Road was a very congested thoroughfare with the 12-ton lorries, local trucks, 10-wheel trailers, pickups, tempos and handcarts servicing the transport companies' warehouses that lined it. They also serviced the wharves such as Indira Dock, Princess Dock, and the Central Railway's freight stations like Wadi Bunder and Carnac Bunder. Everywhere, there was smoke, dust and noise.

Sometimes, Penkar would suddenly point towards something and say, "Look there, look at that." In the blink of an eye, four or five teenagers would clamber up onto the back of a truck, gather whatever goods they can lay their hands on and hurl them by the side of the road. They would then jump off the speeding lorry and make good their escape. By the time the driver or the cleaner noticed anything amiss and came around the back to investigate, there would be no trace of the boys or the stolen goods. Nothing seemed to faze them – not verbal warnings, nor threats of physical violence. The purloined goods would quickly make their way into one of the nearby huts and disappear for good. They seemed to target all kinds of stuff – huge iron girders, angles, scrap materials. Everything was fair game.

One day, three rolls of quarter inch thick copper wire (each roll weighing a hundred kilos) was dragged into their compound and converted into cash within minutes. Penkar said that it went for three thousand rupees. The actual price was thirty-eight rupees a kilo. When the police arrived half an hour later to investigate, there was neither hide nor hair to be seen.

On another day, as Shanmugam, Penkar and Raut were watching, an oil tanker inched along the road amidst heavy traffic and came to a halt at a signal light. A man ran behind it and opened the tap at the back of the tanker. Diesel oil two inches thick bubbled out. Within minutes, men, women and children brought plastic buckets, water pots, cooking vessels and every other type of receptacle and walked off with containers brimming with oil. When the signal changed, the man closed the tap and the vehicle went on its way trailing oil behind it.

One evening, while returning home after work, he saw two sacks full of green peas lying by the side of the road and the usual gang of suspects helping themselves generously to their contents. An employee of Mamaji Industries, who was cramming as much as he could fit into his pockets, looked up and smiled sheepishly as Shanmugam passed by. One day it was ten to fifteen sheaves of bananas strewn all over the street. On another, it was sacks of pulses.

They would sometimes target materials coming from foreign countries meant for the Red Cross or other relief organisations for victims of flood or drought. When bundles of clothes meant for such purposes were raided, it would be comical to see Reay Road residents wandering around wearing ill-fitting and totally inappropriate sweaters, overcoats and gowns.

On a hot and dusty day, a man entered the factory in a rush. He had five or six rolls of cloth in his hand. It was polyester shirting material rolled around long cardboard tubes an inch thick. Each roll measured thirty metres. The designs looked attractive and the cloth would have cost 25-30 rupees a metre in a shop. The man who came rushing in was one of the Reay Road regulars who pinched stuff that 'fell' from the backs of passing trucks. His asking price was two hundred rupees per roll. The two supervisors and a few of the workmen pooled their money together, collected two hundred rupees and bought two rolls. The company advanced another two hundred rupees on behalf of the other workers and two more rolls changed hands.

Acharya seemed to be in two minds. He went back and forth with a face that reflected both eagerness and anxiety in equal measure. He opened his leather bag and closed it. He again opened it, took out his wallet, extracted two hundred rupee notes and bought himself two rolls. For a while, he seemed to wonder where to keep them as they were too long to fit into the cupboard. His face again reflected concern. He finally placed it out of sight in a corner of the stores area.

Reuben was busy cutting a roll into lengths of two metres each. No one put in any work that day after 3.00 p.m. As Acharya busily pretended to write something, Reuben came into the stores area.

"Shanmugam, you didn't buy any?"

"No, Reuben."

"You got scared, huh? What about you Penkar sir?"

Penkar gave a small laugh and, alluding to his lonely existence, asked dejectedly, 'Who do I buy it for?' Reuben made a comical gesture at Acharya and went back to his workplace.

Shanmugam spent the rest of the day racking his brains as to how Acharya would transport his rolls back home.

—

He learnt that there was a Tamil association at Matunga. On a Saturday afternoon he found the place after some searching. It was like he had struck gold. The place was full of books and magazines. There were at least twenty thousand books, five thousand of them novels. Members could check out two books at a time. There was an eight-rupee deposit. The annual subscription was twelve rupees. Entry fee was one rupee. Being unable to raise twenty-one rupees at one go, he frequented the place merely to read the magazines there.

He now got to read the Dinamani on a daily basis. On the 7th, when he received his salary, he went there with the requisite cash. The library and reading room were on the first floor. At the end of the floor was a long room with a board that said 'Executive Committee' on its door. Four of five persons could always be seen in the room conversing in English. It was clear from their tone and accent that they were Brahmins. Sometimes there was the clacking noise of a typewriter, other times the ringing of a telephone. Mostly it was chatter.

Shanmugam peeped into the room. There were index cards containing members' details, used coffee cups, and a short, fat man in a dhoti who resembled an accountant behind a desk. He peered at Shanmugam through his glasses and asked abruptly, "What do you want?"

"I want to enrol as a member, sir."

"Why? So you can read Sandilyan?"

"I've already read all his books sir."

"I know your type. You'll keep coming here until you've

finished all of Sandilyan's books and once you're done, you'll collect your money and walk away."

"No, sir."

"I know, I know. Anyway I've run out of application forms. Come back next month."

A thin man, sporting prominent nose hair, seated in front of him gave a faint smile at this exchange. Unsure how to tackle a man who spoke so rudely, Shanmugam turned away in disappointment.

Just then a man, in a silk dhoti, full-sleeved shirt, a sculpted moustache and a shawl over his shoulder,who looked as though he was coming from a political rally, appeared in front of him.

"What's the matter, thambi?" he enquired.

"I came to apply for membership."

"Who's inside? Sundararaman? Did he say he had run out of forms? Sons of bitches. They'd give out forms only to Brahmins. Come with me."

A twinge of pain assailed Shanmugam as he followed the gentleman.

"Hey Sundararaman, give me a membership form!" the man commanded. The fat man looked up.

"That...no...the forms...they have gone for printing...they aren't back yet..."

"Stop bluffing...I'm sure there are at least two hundred forms in your drawer right now. If you don't want people like him to become members, change the name on the board at the entrance right now..."

"That's not it Kavipithan. These people will stay as members only till they have finished reading all of Sandilyan's works.

Thereafter they'll withdraw their money and walk away."

"Then don't stock Sandilyan's works here. Why the hell do you keep on buying them and stacking the shelves with them then? Give me a form now."

Kavipithan took the proffered form, signed his name in the column 'Introduced By' and handed it to Shanmugam. He also said, "Fill it up quickly and pay the fees. Otherwise, the Manager might lock up the office and go home."

Shanmugam paid the money, obtained a receipt and collected two library cards. He also checked out two books the same day.

—

A rumour went about in the company that it was not doing well financially. It appeared that the order they had expected from Century Rayons for a hundred additional winder machines had not come through. It was said that the order had gone to Texforce Company whose machines were far superior in performance to theirs. There was uncertainty in the air. Salaries had been delayed for the last two or three months. Payday was being deferred to the eighth, ninth and even the tenth. And then, only the worker's wages were being paid. Rumour had it that officials had not been paid their salaries for the previous month. Shanmugam just did not get it – how did a private firm find itself in such dire circumstances? Gossip was rife: the owners had stripped the company of all its assets; staff lay-offs were imminent; temporary employees would be the first to go.

Shanmugam began searching for another job. He would look at the ads in the Times of India, write out seven or eight applications for jobs, go to V.T and drop them off at the box at the newspaper's office kept for that purpose. One or two companies called him for interviews. Some even offered him employment. But their offer did not exceed two hundred rupees. Nothing was working out.

Along with Shanmugam, there were seven others who were temporary employees. There was one person in the baking section, another in the painting division and five on the assembly line. He was the only clerk. Head Office was engaged in large-scale downsizing of personnel. Others voluntarily took a two hundred rupee cut in their salaries on the understanding that, once the company's finances stabilized, this cut would be restored and enhanced. They could afford it as each one drew not less than two thousand rupees. All of them had only basic qualifications but had risen to this level. The winds had been favourable and business had prospered resulting in substantial salary increases to each of them over the years.

Following the 'rationalization' at the Head Office, twelve temporary staffers lost their jobs. In Shanmugam's unit, the other seven temporary personnel received their confirmation orders. This meant a basic salary of one hundred and forty rupees plus dearness allowance, which totalled to three hundred and fifteen rupees a month. In Shanmugam's grade, the basic salary would have been two hundred and fifty and, including dearness allowance, he would have received four hundred and twenty-five rupees. Double of what he was currently drawing.

It looked like all the small luxuries he had dreamed of over the past one and a half years were within his grasp now. He could easily send one hundred and fifty rupees home instead of the current fifty. He could even afford to have a hot meal in the mornings before coming to work.

January 1st was the confirmation date the company had decided upon. That meant they would pay arrears up to May netting him eight hundred and seventy-five rupees. He could afford to buy a couple of trousers and shirts and save the balance for a trip home.

They called each one by name and handed them the confirmation letters. Shanmugam waited for his turn. The other seven had collected their letters and left. Perhaps Dikmani was busy with something else. He waited for ten to fifteen minutes. There was a supplier in Dikmani's office. He waited impatiently for the man to leave. He walked restlessly to and fro. He went into Dikmani's office when the supplier departed.

Dikmani looked up.

For several minutes he fussed with the papers on his desk rearranging them needlessly. He avoided Shanmugam's gaze.

"Yes?" he said, finally.

"Sir…my letter…"

"I'm sorry Shanmugam."

Head Office had ratified his proposal to confirm the jobs of the factory workers. But given that they had terminated forty permanent clerks and twelve temporary clerks, Dikmani had not been given the go-ahead to confirm his position. He could understand Shanmugam's feelings and he would try and do something for him as soon as possible. Shanmugam must be patient until then.

Shanmugam feared that he might burst out crying. There was nothing more to say. He wiped his face with his handkerchief and came out. Acharya's demeanour suggested that he knew what had transpired. But Shanmugam did not think he had a hand in it. It was not as though Dikmani would be acting on Acharya's advice on such matters.

Disappointment filled his stomach. He sat for a while frozen with despair. A number of colleagues came by to offer condolence. Reuben came and put his arm around his shoulder.

The peon came and summoned Shanmugam to Dikmani's office.

He washed his face at the sink, drank some water and, composing himself, went to meet Dikmani. This could very well be his last day at work. If so, he resolved to ask if he deserved such treatment.

While a temporary clerk at the Reay Road unit drew two hundred and fifty rupees, the equivalent was six hundred and fifty rupees at the Head Office. If Shanmugam would have been entitled to four hundred and twenty-five rupees upon confirmation, its equivalent would have been seven hundred and ninety rupees at the Head Office. Given this disparity, he would question how their standards applied in his case.

He went and stood once again in front of Dikmani who spoke in a regretful tone. He had had another word with Head Office and there was nothing further to be done at this stage. On his own initiative, he offered Shanmugam an additional fifty rupees a month as transport allowance and urged him to continue his current good work.

Shanmugam stood silent for a short while. He then seemed to have reached a firm decision. In a voice quivering with emotion, he said, "No, thank you sir. Even though my gut tells me I should accept your offer, my head forbids it. I'll wait, thank you sir."

As he came out, his resolve seemed to crumble and then fortify.

He lost his previous liveliness. But his work ethic continued to be strong. He arrived at the workshop before anyone else and worked late after everyone had left. When he finished his own allotted work, he would help Penkar in writing up advices and posting pin cards. He would help count items during inspections. He would mark packed crates. That's when he found out that marking crates was unlike writing on paper with a pen. He had to use a brush to mark the boxes. He would stand at the assembly section and watch the operations there. Even though he knew the names of parts and their catalogue number, he tried to learn their utility and where they came into play at the assembly.

Even though initially Acharya tried to laugh off his efforts, as days went by it began to sound artificial and forced. It was obvious that Shanmugam's efforts rattled him. This enthused Shanmugam further. Reuben also pitched in and taught him a few basic functions in the assembly area.

**8**

One Saturday afternoon, Shanmugam was hanging around the Times of India's office watching the goings-on. Shoulder-high newsprint rolls, four feet in diameter, imported from Finland, were being fed into machines. The paper was first unfurled in the machine like yards of cloth, printed on one side, then the other, followed by three-colour printing carried out one after another. The pages were then folded, stapled and stacked to become individual copies of the Illustrated Weekly of India. He watched the process with fascination for nearly half an hour.

It was only 4.00 p.m. He didn't feel like going back to the chawl that early. The library at the Tamil association would open only at 6.00 p.m. on Saturdays. He had a whole two hours to kill. He walked slowly, crossed the road vigilantly at the signal and went into V.T Station. He paid thirteen paise and bought himself a cup of tea at the tea stall. He didn't feel like loitering around idly any longer. Since it was the second Saturday of that month, the harbour line trains were relatively uncrowded. He thought he would kill some time by getting into one of them, travel all the way to Kurla and return by the same train.

He boarded a train, snagged a window seat and began biting his nails. He would trim his nails only occasionally. When they grew to a certain length and began accumulating dirt underneath, he would bite them off. He found biting the nails of his thumb a tad difficult and so would moisten them with spit beforehand. He couldn't bite his toenails and they were therefore allowed to grow to a certain length.

By the time he had reached the nail on his thumb, someone came and sat next to him. He casually glanced at the person. The face looked somewhat familiar. Not a local acquaintance, but one from back home. Aah...he had it...he was King Kong's cousin...Karuppiah Pillai sir's nephew. Kamatchi... Kamatchinathan...

There was a gooseberry tree at Karuppiah sir's house whose berries were crunchy, tasty and not too tart. When marinated in salt, they would smell heavenly the next morning. But the local boys would never let it fully ripen on the tree. They would clamber up the high, mud compound wall and target the berries. If they were caught raiding the tree by grandpa – Karuppiah sir's father – he'd lambast them. Sir's sister lived with him. If any of the boys called out to her from the other side of the wall and sought her permission to pluck a few berries, she'd say, "All right then, go ahead and pluck four or five...don't pluck the unripe ones and hurry up. Grandpa is having his bath. If he sees you, you're done for."

That's where King Kong grew up. He possessed enormous girth. Hence the name. Or rather the nickname. He was two years younger than Shanmugam. His vertical growth stopped by age twelve. To make up for it, he grew sideways. His voice cracked. Hair sprouted on his chest, armpits and face as though he was a thirty-year old. At twelve he had had to call on the services of the village barber, Bhagawathy, who lathered and shaved his face. He stayed away from all the other boys in the village, scared of being ridiculed.

Everywhere he went – whether to the temple or to bathe in the river – King Kong would take grandpa along with him for protection. Even though the local boys steered clear of them, scared of grandpa's full-throated abuses, you could hear the hail, 'Hey King Kong' from street corners and from behind trees. Even though grandpa accompanied him up to the school gates, he still had to sit in the classroom with the rest of his compatriots. While the presence of a teacher was somewhat of a deterrent, toilet breaks and lunch breaks offered them the opportunity to pull his legs unmercifully. At such times, he would threaten them in his cracked voice, "I'll tell grandpa…" If pushed too hard, he would grab hold of his tormentor and crush him till his ribs creaked. No one could take him on in one-to-one combat. He'd pulverise the opposition.

Kamatchi used to come to his uncle's house during his school holidays. Shanmugam had met him on many occasions during such visits. He'd last seen him four or five years ago.

"Excuse me…aren't you King Kong's cousin?"

"Yes…and you are…?"

"I'm from Kurungulam. Weren't you a regular visitor to Karuppiah sir's house?"

"Oh, yes. Now I remember. You belong to the sheepherders' community there, don't you?" He immediately bit his tongue realising his faux pas and continued quickly to cover up his gaffe. "Now I remember. I've even come to your house to buy milk. Wasn't there a Curry tree in front of your house? Is it still there?"

"Oh, yes."

"Where are you employed? I work as a typist at Himalayan Instrument Company on Palton Road. Drop in someday. When did you come to Bombay? Uncle had written to say grandpa was suffering from some kind of stomach ailment for quite a while. I don't know if he's recovered yet. My other cousin, Aramboly aunt's son, got married last month. I couldn't go to the wedding obviously…it's not exactly in our backyard, is it? But I'm planning to go home during Diwali." Kamatchi went on and on.

In the course of his monologue, he took Shanmugam along with him to Chembur. They got off at Kurla, bought two tickets, boarded the Mankhurd local and got off at Chembur.

He talked non-stop all the way: news about his uncle back home, stories about another relative at Colaba, with whom he had stayed for two years and then had parted ways following a spat, how that man's younger brother had assaulted him, the Sivaji Ganesan movie he had recently seen at Sagar theatre…

They got off at Chembur station, walked along the train tracks for a while and crossed the level crossing to enter the Shell Colony road. Small shops built of tin sheets and roofed with asbestos lined both sides of the road. They carried on a wide variety of trades: cement, bricks, timber, steel, furniture, utensils, textiles, firewood, pawn shops, eateries, vegetables, laundry, barber shop, stove repair, country liquor, paan, beedi and cigarettes, tea stall.

They went past a flyover and turned into a lane where a row of huts stood. Like the hundreds of colonies commonly found in Bombay's suburbs, lined with huts along the sides of railway tracks, this was Chembur's Indira Nagar.

As they crossed the railway line, there was an open yard with three huts on either side and one hut on the opposite end. There was a puddle at the back of the hut, like a muddled speck of mud left behind by the retreating sea. There was a narrow lane leading to the puddle.

Kamatchi opened the door to the third hut on the left-hand side, and let him in.

The inside was reasonably clean. At a corner straight ahead was a cot. On the left was a table used for cooking. There were two stoves and a few aluminium utensils on the top and, on the lower shelf, a rolling pin and board, bottles containing spices, two tall biscuit tins holding wheat flour and rice. A metal wire container hanging in one corner contained potatoes and onions. Directly underneath it was the wash area. It had a large water drum, two plastic buckets, a mug and a two-litre tin can with a wire handle for carrying water to the toilet.

There were a few calendars on the wall – Murugan, MGR, Jayalalitha. There were a few incense sticks that had burnt to a nub under the picture of Lord Murugan. Three bed rolls were rolled up and shoved under the cot. The cot had a pillow and a blanket on it while a clothesline strung over one corner sported trousers, shirts and towels.

Kamatchi invited him to sit on the bed.

"What time is it?"

"Four forty-five."

"Give me a minute. I'll go and get some milk. We can have tea then."

"No, thanks. I need to go. I'm in a rush."

"There's no rush. Let everyone get back. Stay for dinner. The others will return one by one. Shenbagam has gone to attend to his rice business and will be back only after five. His younger brother, Muthu Nadar, works in a shop. It'll be almost nine by the time he returns. Sit down, I'll be back in a jiffy."

He crossed the railway line, went into a shop, bought some milk, and brewed tea. He poured some in a glass for Shenbagam and kept it aside.

Shanmugam knew Kamatchi's parents. They belonged to the Saiva Vellalar community. They used to come to Shanmugam's house to purchase milk. Kamatchi's mother used to address Appa as 'anne'. Since it was a small village, everyone seemed to be related to everyone else. They used to participate in each other's family functions such as marriages, but the Vellalars wouldn't eat at others' houses. It was therefore customary to send supplies like rice, pulses, vegetables and so on to their houses one day before the ceremony. When it came to public functions, like temple festivals, where everybody belonging to all the eighteen castes was fed, the Saiva Vellalars were served first and ate separately by themselves.

Kamatchi's father was a jobber at the carding section of R. V. Mills. A committed communist, he read a lot. Whenever he came to the village on holidays, he would spread his towel and lie down after lunch at the Sathankoil veranda with a book by either S. A. Dange or A. K. Gopalan in his hand. Once, while there was a strike at R.V. Mills, he had stayed at their village for two whole months. Shanmugam had interacted with him during that period. While others argued superficially about politics, he would quote reams of statistics in support of his statements.

Kamatchi mentioned that his father would be retiring this year and that Paramasivam, which was King Kong's actual name, would take up that job after him. As they were chatting, Shenbagam walked in.

After introductions, when Shanmugam tried once again to take his leave, they wouldn't allow it.

The conversation continued along with the prep work for the night's dinner. The advance for that accommodation was one hundred rupees and the rent, forty rupees. Three persons were currently sharing it.

Including food, the total monthly expenses would amount to somewhere between one hundred and one hundred and fifty rupees. There would be tea and chapattis in the morning. For lunch, you could carry packed chapattis and a curry. At night, there would be rice and sambar. Shenbagam and Muthu were non-vegetarians. They would cook fish or meat at least once a week. On those days, Kamatchi would prepare a separate vegetable dish for himself.

There was place for one more person.

No riff-raff allowed.

Shenbagam was grinding spices for the curry. Rice was cooking on the stove. Kamatchi and Shanmugam peeled onions and garlic. In honour of Shanmugam annachi's visit, it had been decided that they would make a spicy sambar with garlic and shallots, accompanied by roast pappad. Shanmugam quickly warmed up to Shenbagam. His speech was artless and laughter genuine.

'Why not move in here with them?' thought Shanmugam. He could help them with the cooking. He could read whenever the urge seized him. It felt close and friendly, like a proper home.

"What do you do for water?"

"There's a Tamilian who lives just across the train tracks. He has water supply round the clock at his place. We take our buckets there and fetch water for our use. We pay him five rupees a month for it. You can bathe in the wash area, or else, there are two flagstones behind the house. You can stand on them and pour water over yourself."

"What about latrine facilities?"

Kamatchi laughed and said, "You have to carry that tin of water and go to the railway tracks to do your business. You must go before dawn or else wait till twilight when the place won't be too crowded. When trains pass by, you either turn your face away or cover it with a towel or an umbrella."

When Shanmugam used to travel by the 8.30 a.m. train from Mahim, he had seen women defecating along the tracks near Wadala Road railway station. If you were reluctant to do your business near the tracks where trains plied every three minutes, you would have to wait there the whole day. The women would therefore squat there with the water cans in front of them, their sari folds covering their private parts, keeping their heads down or shielding their faces with an umbrella.

Men, on the other hand, seemed unconcerned, as they smoked their beedis casually and watched the trains. They would, in general, appear quite relaxed.

Night times were perhaps the best. But you need to be watchful of train movements all the time. It was always advisable to walk facing an oncoming train.

For these visits, you needed to purchase a separate pair of plastic slippers. You also needed to wash your feet before re-entering the house.

During monsoons, there would be waterlogging everywhere, leaving only the top of the train tracks exposed. Water would also accumulate in front of the hut. What then?

Kamatchi said, "You need to adjust, annachi. For us men, it's not much of a problem. We don't care if people stare at us. Imagine the plight of the women! Some of them do their business indoors on newspapers spread out on the floor which they then dispose of when no one's around."

Shanmugam was aghast when he heard this.

After dinner, Shenbagam suggested, "Why not move in with us, annachi?"

Kamatchi seconded the motion enthusiastically, "Yes annachi. Vacate your present accommodation on the First of next month and come over here."

Shanmugam found himself with no ready response to their invitation.

—

Lakshmi and her husband lived in the first of the three houses across them. A Brahmin, she was married to Jayapandian Nadar who worked at a grocery store. This surprised Shanmugam. How could a Brahmin marry a Nadar? It obviously wasn't a case of kidnapping, for she wasn't kept under lock and key. Could it be love? If so, could love transcend caste and community lines?

Like everyone else, Shanmugam also addressed her as Lakshmi akka. Lakshmi akka was pregnant. In the evenings, when she had finished all her chores, she would wash her face, comb her hair, apply a vermillion dot on her forehead and sit at the entrance to their house reading the Ananda Vikatan or Kalaimagal awaiting Nadar's return from work. She would also borrow the books that Shanmugam brought home from the library.

The next house was occupied by four Malayali youths. Two of them, paternal cousins, claimed to be motor mechanics. The other two, having obtained their passports, were awaiting visas to migrate to either Saudi Arabia or Abu Dhabi.

In the last house in the row was a fifty-year old woman, her son who studied at the local Municipal school and her plump daughter who was around twenty or twenty-five years of age, whose marital status was uncertain. Whether she was unmarried, separated, divorced, or widowed no one knew for sure. The mother was employed at the naval hospital, INHS Asvini, in Colaba, probably in some menial capacity. She'd leave at dawn and return by 4.30 or 5.00 in the evening, carrying a bulging cloth bag. The daughter would receive a severe tongue-lashing immediately upon the mother's return. Either the dishes would remain unwashed or the house would not have been cleaned. The mother's diatribe would reflect her own defeat and powerlessness. But nothing seemed to penetrate Annammai's thick skin or faze her.

The lone house that faced the yard was vacant ever since the previous occupants had vacated it a month ago.

The first house in Shanmugam's line was occupied by a Muslim family from Peranampattu in Tamil Nadu. Shanmugam was yet to lay eyes on the man of the house. He also never could find out when the man left for work and when he returned home. The lady, with a baby in her arms, was pregnant again. She had one of those bright, angelic faces that would lift anybody's spirits. Whenever she greeted him saying, 'Hello thambi,' the warmth in her words was very evident.

The third house in their row was home to a Marathi family whose members were employed somewhere in loading and unloading capacities. They were from the plateau region. Most times they would return home only after 10.00 at night and start their cooking thereafter. The hiss of the stove could be heard for a very long time. The smell of garlic being sautéed would hover around the house. Some days the smell of dried shrimp being shallow fried on a wok would rise above the settlement. Shanmugam has gone to sleep many a day to the humming sound of their stove. Even before dawn broke, Champabai would knock on their door and demand, "Hey anna, give me a matchbox," unconcerned that the breasts she had bared to either her baby or her husband the night before were still in full view. The language they spoke, which had earlier sounded merely as loud noises to Shanmugam, had recently begun to make some sense.

Kamatchi was, in a sense, self-absorbed. His own interests came first; everything else took a distant second place. But Shenbagam was different. He was filled with human kindness and it showed.

Bombay was then facing an acute scarcity of rice. A kilo of rice went for over seven rupees. A law was promulgated that hotels and eating houses should not serve rice on Mondays and Wednesdays. Another law forbade feeding over twenty persons at social functions or gatherings.

Some of the Shetty eateries began serving millet in place of rice. Every mouthful of it came with sand. Several restaurants offered cracked parboiled wheat, called 'lapsi', as a substitute. However, its colour and rubbery texture ensured it did not catch on in a big way. To force it down, you needed to douse it liberally with large quantities of sambar or rasam.

There was plenty of demand for rice in the black market, especially in localities like Sion, Koliwada, Matunga, Chembur, Dharavi and Andheri where Tamilians lived in large numbers. There was also a ban on carrying more than five kilos of rice anywhere within the city. To many men, women and children from Salem, the rice trade was their lifeline. Rice had to be brought from places like Trombay, Mumbra, Titiwala or Badlapur on the Central Line or Bassein Road on the Western Railway. The trip to and fro would take about four hours. A mark-up of a rupee per kilo of rice was a reasonable margin.

While it was sold by the kilo, there were no scales or weights. They would use an old Bournvita or a Glaxo tin for measuring purposes. This was acceptable to both parties and the tins themselves were provided by the households purchasing the rice.

They would make two trips in a day. They held season tickets for this purpose. If they encountered RPF personnel or a ticket examiner, they would press a rupee or two into their hands. They would travel as a group and sometimes each would place a handful of rice into the bags being carried by the RPF person or the TTE for this purpose. Occasionally, they would also simply smile, talk their way out and get away with it.

Shenbagam carried out this business in a slightly more sophisticated manner. His appearance – tall, well-built, neatly shaved with a trimmed moustache and well-dressed – aided him in his endeavours. He would carry a neat travel bag, handling it adroitly so as to camouflage its actual weight when boarding and alighting from buses or trains or while walking along the roads.

He was the purveyor of good quality, thin, long rice. He would change trains at Kurla, get off at Mumbra, board a bus for Taloja from where he would procure his stock. He found the prices there reasonable and measures fair. He was able to transport fifteen to twenty kilos per trip. He always had a stock of two-rupee notes to hand out to the 'nuisances' he encountered on the way. He would put on an innocent face and explain he had purchased the stock for his own personal use.

There was no question of measuring or weighing the stock he supplied to his customers. He'd simply say, "Sami, I've got twenty kilos. Give me one hundred and forty rupees." On this basis, he had a regular clientele of some twenty to thirty households. He'd keep aside a kilo of rice separately for their consumption during his evening trip. He'd also purchase vegetables on his way back at Chembur. Kamatchi would grouse that spinach or other greens took a long time to clean. Shenbagam was in charge of the prep work for curries. Kamatchi would do the actual cooking. Dish washing and fetching water were Muthu's chores. Shanmugam pitched in by cutting vegetables, washing and cleaning greens, kneading dough for chapattis and clearing stones and other impurities from the rice.

Everyone ate to their hearts' content. They packed chapattis and curry for their lunch. On Sundays they went out together to watch Tamil movies. However, there was one small hitch – Kamatchi was a Sivaji fan whereas Shenbagam was an ardent devotee of MGR. On occasions they would engage in fierce battles in support of their respective icons.

Shanmugam bought all Tamil weekly magazines. He also had two books from the Tamil Sangam always at hand. This earned him the reputation of being a well-read intellectual. Under the impression that all those reading Kumudam and Vikatan were learned scholars, he earned the privilege to visit the Tamil Sangam as often as he wished.

He would visit the Tamil association every Sunday at 4.00 p.m. without fail. Early visitors to the Sangam enjoyed an additional benefit: they could comfortably use its toilet facilities without any disturbance. On the ground floor there were two toilets, one each for ladies and gents. The first floor contained a western-style commode while the second floor, which had accommodation facilities for guests and visitors, housed a row of latrines. Shanmugam however did not care much for the western-style toilet. When the shit hit the pan with a 'plop', the water in it would sometimes splash onto his butt. That felt disgusting. The one on the ground floor was a squat toilet which he preferred. Even when a private function like a wedding or a reception was being celebrated at the Association, he would boldly barge into the premises and make use of its toilet facilities. On the days he visited the Tamil Sangam, Shanmugam would give the train tracks a miss.

The Sangam's Secretary, Librarian and one or two other regular members were also residents of Chembur. Shanmugam got to know them by sight and also exchanged one or two words with them occasionally. When asked about his residence in Chembur, he grandly mentioned Shell Colony.

Sometimes the Secretary or the Librarian would tell him, "Hold on. I'll come with you." He would somehow try to slough them off. But, after telling them, "I'm actually going to Matunga on an errand," what do you do if they came up briskly behind you and tapped you on your shoulder when you were on your way to Koliwada Station? He'd try to ditch them as soon as they landed at Chembur Station, by either pretending he had to shop for fruits or vegetables or that it was time for his dinner and he had to get to the eatery. Shanmugam took great care not to let anyone know that he lived in one of the huts by the railway tracks.

Since he made the first visit to the train tracks well before dawn, there was no problem. At nights, when illuminated by headlights of passing trains, he'd shrink at the thought that he might be recognised by some acquaintance of his. He would always wear a towel around his head and neck and keep his head down like a bashful bride.

He would wake up very early most mornings. Some Sundays, however, they would all sleep in. And by the time they woke up, the sun would also be up. It would not be possible for Shanmugam to visit the train tracks then. He would try to hold it in as long as possible, but this was not something that could be held back for a very long time. He would therefore put on his shirt and pant, collect his season ticket and some change and go to the station. Chembur Station had no facilities to offer. He'd therefore travel all the way to Kurla, wait in line at the station's latrines, ask the bhangi to pour water and clear the mess left behind by the previous customer, fill a tin can with water and squat down.

Even then it would require some advance preparations: fold the trouser to the knees, unfasten the belt, unbutton the trouser, push the underpants down...

Before he could complete, a knock would be heard on the door and a loud voice would say, "Chalo jaldi, let's go number three…hurry up number two…"

Thinking he had taken too long, he would push and strain harder to finish quickly causing himself pain.

It was only later he found out that the knock was not directed exclusively at him. It was customary to knock on every door after a while to hurry things along. He had also heard that the same practice was followed at all the cheap brothels in the city. If the doorman, and the prostitute under you constantly kept chivvying, how were you expected to complete your screwing?

Each knock would cause him panic. And that would only prolong his time inside. But there were other incentives to quicken his departure and finish as fast as he could. The stink of excrement, the stench of urine, the creepy cockroaches that stuck their feelers out of the cracks in the door, the wriggly worms, the sudden bursting of noisome bubbles in the toilet bowl sending up an unholy reek, the dead intestinal worms lying around, the phlegm hawked up by previous users…The Railway Minister, Board Members, General Managers, Heads of Traffic, Technical and Commercial personnel, each one of them deserved to be locked up in these cubicles for a few hours.

He would come out, wash his hands, tip the bhangi and exit the station. For some reason all the attendants at these toilets spoke Gujarati.

For the first few Sundays, Kamatchi, Shenbagam and Muthu wondered where annachi went in the mornings. Once they found out, every time Shanmugam would get ready to leave, there would be much hilarity in the hut.

And when inevitably everyone in their compound got to know about this practice, they began pulling his legs too. "So, off to the toilet, eh?" they would tease.

Kamatchi suffered from hemorrhoids. If piles occurred, he would suffer terrible pain until it subsided. He treated the condition with herbal medicines. He also avoided spicy food. He would help himself sparingly to sambar and pick out green chillies from the curries. He always kept a half-litre bottle of sesame oil separately for his own use. Bananas were bought from the common fund. Shenbagam and Muthu required their food to be reasonably spicy. So did Shanmugam. If spicy sambar was on the menu, the next day would be tough. It would entail two visits to the tracks in the morning. Or, if it was a Sunday, he would have to make two trips to Kurla Station.

Saturdays were half days for Shanmugam. He had days off on bank holidays. The others did not enjoy this perk. Time would then hang heavy on his hands. He would be home by 1.30 p.m. on Saturdays, have his lunch and lie down to read. Sometimes he'd nod off. The door would be open with the entrance covered by a hessian curtain. It would let in light and an occasional visitor.

The Brahmin akka would come for a chat. She'd prop the curtain over the door, sit at the entrance with her back against the door, her legs stretched out and, supporting her stomach carefully, chat with him. Or they would simply read magazines together in companionable silence. He had long wanted to ask her about the mystery behind her marriage. If the Muslim lady came for a visit, she'd stand at the entrance holding on to the door and talk. However, her visits were short-lived as she had her hands full with her little one.

Annammai's visits were always sudden and unexpected. Her behaviour was also peculiar. She'd simply stand and stare. Her accent was pure Salem. She did not have the habit of reading. She was interested in movies and that was about it.

Even though many weeklies were strewn around, she'd snatch the one in Shanmugam's hands. She'd leaf through it cursorily, fling it back at him and leave. Her departures were also equally precipitate. He didn't know what to do with her. His mind would be in turmoil for as long as she was in the hut with him.

On bank holidays, Annammai would drop in after everyone had gone to work and the Brahmin and Muslim akkas had laid down for a nap after their morning chores. She would not stand or sit at the doorstep or lift up the door curtain. She would simply barge in and try to make some conversation. She would leaf through the magazines and look at the pictures in them.

Annammai had a big build. She sported an impressive pair of breasts. Her body odour would be overpowering if she dropped in before she had had a bath. Some nights, he would imagine her presence alongside him. On his days off, he would await Annammai's arrival with some trepidation. His heart would beat wildly—'Here she comes, she'll be here any moment'. He wouldn't be able to concentrate on whatever he was reading. He would feel feverish with anticipation. As time went by, the fever would peak and it would subside slowly once she had come and gone. On the days she did not visit him, time would seem to crawl.

Once the dread passed, the feverish lull seemed almost pleasant. His mind began craving more and more. All his earlier aversions about her ugliness dissipated and he began appreciating those traits.

Both seemed to have plenty to think about. Who will initiate the first move? This seemed to be a silent game between them. Sometimes when Annammai came in, Shanmugam would pretend to be fast asleep with a book across his chest. There would initially be the sound of her entry but then she'd leave quietly without a trace.

He couldn't seem to decide. Fear was the major inhibitor. He did not worry about Shenbagam, Kamatchi or Muthu. What if the Brahmin or the Muslim akka walked in? To earn the wrath of Annammai's loud-mouthed mother was one thing. But to have the veneer of a 'gentleman' stripped away forever was a nightmare.

Despite these factors, the obsession with sex overwhelmed him.

One Saturday afternoon, Shanmugam got off at Chembur, walked some distance through an unfamiliar road, and looked for a petty shop that seemed deserted. Extremely self-conscious, he looked around in all directions and bought a packet of condoms.

# 9

Shenbagam has been missing for two days. He hadn't returned from his rice run. He would normally have been home by seven or eight o'clock at the latest. Where could he have gone? Kamatchi and Shanmugam decided to go ahead with their dinner preparations assuming he was simply delayed somewhere. They also waited a while before having their dinner. Shenbagam's portion was set aside.

They must have dozed off. When Shanmugam woke up in the middle of the night, nothing was visible in the pitch darkness. A flock of cockroaches, disturbed by something, was fluttering around the hut. When his eyes adjusted to the darkness, Shenbagam's sleeping slot was still empty. His heart jolted.

He got up, groped around for the matchbox, struck a light and looked at the clock. Two forty. Where could Shenbagam have gone?

All kinds of dire scenarios began to run through his mind. Each day, at least four or five commuters travelling by the overcrowded local trains lose their lives by hanging precariously out of the coaches. They lose their grip and fall or get hit by electric poles. A number of people are also run over by trains while trying to cross the railway tracks. Several merely lose their limbs, while some are dissected into two and die at the spot, twitching in agony. Some corpses are found with no external injuries, but with blood trickling out of their ears.

The bodies continue to lie at the spot until the beedi-smoking railway coolies bring out their blood-stained canvas stretchers and reach the accident site.

Thick-skinned commuters, inured to such sights, simply give these gruesome visions a fleeting look, a sideways glance or a horrified stare before carrying on to their workplaces. Those who are injured, die while lying on the stretchers waiting for the next train. Otherwise, they expire on the way to the hospital or pass away while they are dumped on the veranda of the Byculla Railway Hospital or the Thane Civil Hospital. The fortunate few walk or hobble out with missing arms or legs.

Even though Shenbagam was not the kind to footboard, there were a million ways one could get injured or hurt. Or perhaps the Civil Supplies guys had caught hold of him while he was bringing his rice in. If he fell into their hands and they did not accept his two rupee 'sweetener', they would merely confiscate his stock, knock him around a bit and let him go. They would then share the rice among themselves. Or else, they would detain him for a day and then let him go. This seemed likely. Shenbagam was not the sort to spend his nights elsewhere without informing them. He was a very responsible person. He had a maternal uncle living in Govandi but visited him only rarely.

Till twelve years of age, he had grown up in the lap of luxury and love. He had gone to a missionary school at Valliyur, four miles from his town, by means of a horse-drawn carriage. His father was a very influential Thevar in the entire area. Family feuds had resulted in murders. When Shenbagam's father was arrested red-handed with a pistol in his possession, seven deaths had taken place on both sides. After four years of litigation, by which time all their money and possessions had been drained, the government carried out the eighth killing.

Shanmugam has seen a family portrait of Shenbagam that included his father, mother, two sisters and two brothers. Shenbagam's mother wore a thick necklace, earrings, eardrops and a thali, all made of gold. He couldn't even begin to imagine what she must look like these days. The family was now subsisting on what Shenbagam and Muthu managed to send home each month and a small plot of land on which they grew groundnuts and horse gram.

The elder sister had been married off and Shenbagam was planning to sell either the small piece of land or their home within the next one or two years. With the proceeds, he would carry out his younger sister's wedding. Apparently her complexion was as fair as their mother's. She also owned three lambs. Sometimes when Shenbagam was on about her, Shanmugam would begin to wonder whether he should offer to marry her himself. This fleeting thought would simultaneously trigger a cynical smile. Who knew what exorbitant sums his appa would demand as dowry? A vulgar saying about God and his priest would then come to his mind: while God himself was reduced to masturbating, his priest prayed for a wet, hot cunt!

The thought occupied his mind as he put on his slippers, went towards the tracks, urinated and turned homewards.

A cloudless sky. A crescent moon. The clatter of trains that could be heard throughout the day was missing. He sat for a while on the train tracks feeling very worried. Where could Shenbagam have gone? Finally, he returned home to await the morning and see if it would bring Shenbagam back. But sleep evaded him. He waited, hoping to hear Shenbagam's footsteps approaching.

In the morning, Kamatchi suggested they wait till that night. They went off to work with heavy hearts. Muthu was drained of colour. Shenbagam did not return the next day either. Muthu went to inform his uncle.

They began searching in earnest the next morning. They visited hospitals, morgues, detention centres where ticketless travellers were normally held and a few police stations en route but in vain.

The whole thing was a mystery. Somehow, they felt responsible for his disappearance. They had no idea how to proceed further. They didn't write home to inform his family members concerned that it might worry them unnecessarily. They submitted a police complaint. His uncle suggested they wait a few more days for developments.

The weather was hot, humid and sweaty. During train journeys, the baniyan would soak up the body's sweat and let off a stink when removed in the evenings. Sleep did not come easily at nights. They put up a small canopy in the yard using coconut thatch. Some slept under it in the open in order to catch the slightest breeze. But the breeze, when it came, brought with it all the dust particles in the world. How does one get a goodnight's rest in such circumstances?

Either the heat or the strain of all the running around made Muthu complain for two days of tiredness, a heavy head and high fever. He also suffered tremendous bodily pain. On the third day, small berry-like eruptions began sprouting on his forehead. His face was flushed and lips became dry and cracked.

They tied bunches of neem leaves at the entrance to their hut. They burnt incense inside the house. The neighbours looked in and passed on their recommended home remedies. The highest standard of cleanliness must be maintained. There was no need to panic. No non-vegetarian dishes should be cooked. No roasting mustard seeds or papadam. Muthu should not be given anything hot to eat or drink. He needed food that had a cooling effect on the body like coconut water, bananas, cold gruel with Madras onions, yogurt, and ice apple.

The fever should subside first. Once that happens, there was nothing to fear. He should be careful not to scratch the itchy blisters with his hands. He should use the neem leaves for this purpose. He should also not pop the blisters. If he does, they may leave a permanent scar. Left to themselves, the lesions would dry up and the scabs would fall off on their own. He would be allowed to bathe only then. He should boil neem leaves and turmeric, apply a paste of them on his body and use the cooled medicated water to bathe in. He was allowed to come out of the hut only after he has had three such baths. Till then, he should stay cloistered at home.

It was pitiable to watch Muthu. He lost a lot of weight. The untamed ferocity in his eyes had given way to calmness. Self-quarantine was enforced. He would be given bread and milk in the mornings. They would prepare gruel and keep it aside for him to have in the afternoons before they left for work. The Brahmin and Muslim akkas were pregnant and it was therefore not advisable for them to look in on him often. When her mother wasn't around, Shanmugam mentioned this to Annammai privately.

Every time Shanmugam reached home in the evenings he would have his heart in his mouth. Only after he peered into the house and saw Muthu asleep with his chest moving up and down with each breath, or simply lying down staring at nothing, would he feel relieved.

On the very first day of Muthu's sickness, Kamatchi, citing the unbearable heat inside the hut, rolled up his bedding and went to sleep in the yard. It was quite evident though that the heat was not the sole reason for his move.

He lowered the wick in the lamp and went to bed, but sleep was hard to come by. All kinds of fears and doubts kept assailing him. This was a highly contagious disease. He could also contract it. If he did, he would also be laid up for ten to fifteen days. He would miss work on those days and lose wages. Would they use it as an excuse to sack him? Maybe he should get vaccinated. Was a vaccine available for chickenpox?

The blisters began to crust and scab over. The scabs began falling off. Muthu would go out late at night to the train tracks after draping a piece of cloth over his head and covering his face. He wasn't supposed to. But what else was the alternative?

The hut was thoroughly cleaned and aired out. Incense was lit and by the time they finished spraying disinfectant, Muthu came back from his bath. It was a Sunday. Kamatchi went about preparing the day's meal in a leisurely manner. He prepared a dal the bhaiyas were known to make, with garlic, onions, tomatoes, ginger, coriander leaves and potatoes. There was raw onion on the side. A sense of relief ran through the day's meal. But underneath it was the continuous hum of agony over not knowing Shenbagam's whereabouts.

On the twenty-first day since his disappearance, Shenbagam returned home. He had been reduced to skin and bones with protruding cheekbones, a shaggy beard and matted hair infested with lice.

It was late in the evening of a working day. Everyone was busy preparing the next meal when a shadow loomed over the entranceway. They couldn't believe their eyes.

Only his eyes reflected a glimmer of life.

Kamatchi ran and clutched his hands. As soon as the initial shock faded, everyone began speaking at once. He borrowed three rupees and went and had his hair cut. Having bathed, he lit incense sticks and prayed in front of Lord Muruga.

He had been caught by the Special Squad while returning after buying rice. They kept him in remand for two days and then sent him to Yerawada jail, whose most famous inmate had been Mahatma Gandhi. His jail sentence of thirty days had been commuted to twenty days when he agreed to donate blood.

Shanmugam went to the shop and bought eggs. When Shenbagam tried to grind spices for the curry, Kamatchi asked him to take it easy for another day. Everyone from the compound came to enquire about his well-being. The Brahmin lady brought him a glass of tea. "What? Nothing for us, akka?" Kamatchi teased her. Annammai came hiding behind her mother, and secretly made faces at Shanmugam.

The house suddenly seemed brighter.

After dinner, when they were all preparing to go to bed, Shenbagam asked Shanmugam, "Annachi, can you arrange a hundred rupees for me?"

He was under compulsion to return to his rice trade. There were still a few days left before Shanmugam's salary was due. He had about thirty rupees on hand. Even if he gave it away, what about the balance? And what would he do for his own expenses till the next payday? Could he take a loan from someone in his office? But who would be ready and willing to provide him one? Even if they did, he would have to return it as soon as he received his salary.

Then he remembered the Henri Sandoz watch presented to him by his appa at his graduation.

"I'll let you have the money tomorrow evening," said Shanmugam.

—

Rains began to lash the city. The first showers washed the dust off the streets, the roofs of buildings and the leaves on the trees. It was wet and damp all around. Earthworms jutted out everywhere like root-tips of banyan trees. Men propped up signs reading 'Danger' at various spots and opened up manhole covers in the middle of the roads. Muddy water eddied and flowed.

Leaves, polythene sheets, rubber slippers, fruit peels all tumbled down together. Rain kept falling intermittently. The damp smell inside the train coach was indescribable. Dripping umbrellas and raincoats, droplets falling off shaken heads, sticky polyester shirts, mist-like rain blown in by the wind…

The hut also leaked. On one of his days off, Shenbagam brought a large piece of polythene sheet and fitted it tightly to the roof by means of ropes. The house also gave off a musty smell. Was it from the wet sack covering the door, from the thatched roof or the wall? It was an unusual odour peculiar to cockroach infestation.

Once you returned home, you didn't feel like going out again. There was ankle-deep mud in the yard. You had to wash your feet at the entrance and wipe it on a piece of sack before entering the hut. There was a large puddle at the back of the huts. The water level threatened to rise and drown the train tracks at any moment. The huts were said to be built at a higher level than the tracks. But still, the sound of the water in the backyard when heard through the walls was ominous. If the mud embankment broke, the back of the hut would flood. The water had nowhere else to go.

If the mornings were filled with the sound of frogs croaking and cockroaches parading around, nights were the time for bedbugs. On the request of the others, Shanmugam had slept on the cot for two nights. The bedbug bites were sufficient to send him scrambling. He was left with thick welts on his body as though caterpillars had crawled all over it. He couldn't get a proper night's rest. All he had left to show for it was the mouldy, unpleasant smell of the bugs he had squashed throughout the night. From the third night onwards, he opted to sleep on the floor along with the rest of them. Muthu took the cot. It seemed that the bedbugs did not bother him. Do they target only certain blood types or were they only attracted to the smell of certain bodies? Unfortunately for him, Shanmugam would start squirming as soon as he sat on station benches, cinema seats or railway berths. It would seem that a fortunate few were totally immune to bedbug bites.

On the floor, next to the cot, lay Shenbagam, then Kamatchi and finally, near the doorway, Shanmugam. Kamatchi had the annoying habit of putting his hand or leg over the person sleeping next to him with a heavy thump. This would cause that person to wake up frequently with a start and fling the offending limb away. In the mornings he would ask, "Why did you wrestle with me all of last night?"

One day, just before daybreak, Shanmugam found something curled up near his feet. He struck a match – he always kept a matchbox handy – and a small dog, just out of puppyhood, lifted its head and gazed back at him. He opened the door and let it out. The board at the bottom of the door had cracked a few days back. He brought out the cutting boards, propped them up against the crack and went back to bed. He found the pup again the next night asleep near his knee. Since it was raining, he didn't have the heart to toss the little pest out again. But its proximity was revolting. He made a mental note to ask Shenbagam to fix the broken door the next day, but the matter kept slipping his mind.

He didn't see the dog in the morning. Even if he did, he probably wouldn't have recognised it. Its appearance however reminded him of the dog he had killed back in his village.

Four or five years ago, Shanmugam and the cowherd Yesu Adiyan had killed a young dog. Shanmugam had got hold of a small pup and brought it home to guard the house, cattle shed and their land. It whimpered a lot initially and took some time to settle down. He bought a collar, a chain and an aluminium dish for it to eat and drink from.

All pups are cuddly and pretty to begin with. As the pup grew older, its white coat turned brindle and its round face became elongated. It barked incessantly. It pooped indiscriminately everywhere. It would also lift its leg and urinate all over the grinding stone. It would enter the kitchen when no one was around and upend all the vessels looking for leftovers. It was easy enough to pick up a stick and threaten the animal when it unleashed such mayhem at your home. But what do you do when it recreates the same havoc at your neighbours' houses? To top it all, it had bit two youngsters in the village.

The pup had turned into a massive nuisance. Why did they have to field complaints about its behaviour from all the townsfolk? Appa and Amma blamed Shanmugam and held him responsible for all the dog's misdeeds. Fed up with their nagging, Shanmugam stuffed the pup into a sack and handed it to Velandi who accustomed the mountains to grub for tubers. Before he could sigh in relief at the riddance, it was back home the next evening all covered in dust, trying to lick his face enthusiastically. He was terribly upset. If it wasn't such a pest, it could stay. But it made his existence hell.

Four houses down the street from Shanmugam's was the house of Krishna Konar. There was a long history of enmity between the two families. The situation was so fraught that they wouldn't even offer condolences to each other in case of deaths in their respective families. While Shanmugam would move aside and give way on the street if he caught sight of anyone from their family, Krishna Konar's son, Balaraman, would deliberately hawk and spit on the road whenever he spied any of their family members.

Balaraman was seven or eight years older than Shanmugam. When Shanmugam was at school, Balaraman had already begun herding sheep and milking cows. In the process, he had gone up and down hills, mountains, forests and groves and this had endowed him with a well-muscled body. He would sport a thick bamboo staff, with his dhoti hitched up to show his underwear, a sickle tucked into his waist, a jaunty turban wound around his head and a luxuriant moustache lovingly grown and carefully nourished.

Even though the cause for the discord was lost in the mists of time, and was probably something insignificant, the feud had only worsened after Balaraman burst into the scene. There were a lot more disputes and arguments than ever before. When Balaraman would stand in the street railing against them, the members of the Ramaswamy Konar family would go into their house, close the door and play a Telugu station on their radio loud enough to drown out the vulgar tirade outside.

"Come out of the house and face me if you're a real man… motherfucker! I'll disembowel you today…going to college and putting on airs…do you think you're better than me?" yelled Balaraman at Shanmugam the day the dog had barked at him.

Shanmugam didn't know what to do. It was no use trying to tie the dog up. It'd either slip the collar and run off or set up a loud howling that would bother the entire village. The very next day, it barked at Balaraman again. It wasn't clear if it didn't care for Balaraman's personality or for the stench of rotgut that emanated from his mouth. This set off another round of obscene tirade by Balaraman in front of their house.

That was when Shanmugam decided to get rid of the dog. There was leftover insecticide— Folidol—at home after the crops had been sprayed. He put some rice on the aluminium dish, poured the remaining Folidol over it and covered the whole thing with a generous dollop of fish curry and added a fish head to the dish, which he then ceremoniously placed in front of the dog. It delicately picked up just the fish head and ate it with great finesse. It didn't even sniff the rice. Shanmugam was enraged. In his frustration, he picked up a stick and gave the dog a few lusty blows which only resulted in its pissing all over the yard.

The next day was a Sunday. After consultations with Yesu Adiyan, he tied a piece of coir rope around the dog's neck and led it to the fields. There he yanked the rope tighter and tighter around its neck as it squealed in agony until his own innards quaked. It planted its paws stiffly on the ground, resisting his tugging. They quickly pulled it towards a hole that Yesu Adiyan had already dug at the foot of a dwarf coconut palm, shoved it inside and piled soil and dirt over it, all the time wondering if the dog was dead or whether he should dig it out again.

He lost his appetite for four or five days thereafter. He didn't go towards the fields either. He felt a sort of self-loathing. When the chickens scratched at the foot of the coconut plant, clumps of dog hair were unearthed.

When, after some time, the coconut palm began yielding nuts, the dog's memory once again unsettled him.

This pup seemed to revive that memory by turning up every night by his side.

# **10**

Kamatchi was going home to attend his younger brother's wedding. Shanmugam accompanied him to Dadar Station to see him off. His heart began to ache with longing. When would he be able to make his way back home? As Kamatchi outlined his itinerary– reach Chennai the next day, catch the Nellai Express from there, arrive at Papanasam the day after, and take a dip in the Thamirabarani River–Shanmugam's heart heated up even more.

Kamatchi went on talking non-stop, sparing no thought for his own abject state citing which his younger brother's marriage was fixed ahead of his.

When the realisation suddenly dawned that it had been two years since he left home, Shanmugam could not help but feel overwhelmed. He had no clue when he would be able to make his own getaway.

There were absolutely no signs that his job was going to be made permanent any time soon. Currently, he subsisted on an arrangement where he would borrow twenty or thirty rupees each month to be returned on salary days. Under such circumstances, it would take an entire month of Sundays before he could accumulate a thousand rupees and make his trip home.

Maybe he should have signed up for a chit fund scheme contributing twenty-five rupees a month which paid out five hundred rupees, and saved himself this mental agony. The office had recently started deducting twenty-six rupees as Provident Fund contribution and twelve rupees towards Employees State Insurance premium from his pay. Where was he going to find an additional twenty-five rupees?

Reuben Joseph suggested, "Why don't you give tuitions in the evenings or take up part-time employment like typewriting or accounts work?" There were a lot of people who did so.

He looked around a couple of places, but nothing worked out. It'd be easier if someone reliable recommended him. He again sought Iyer's assistance and through him met a Gujarati seth. He lived at King's Circle and had a son in the 9th grade and a daughter in the 7th. It was agreed that Shanmugam would teach them subjects like English, Maths and Science for a monthly salary of sixty rupees.

He would teach them from six to seven-thirty in the evenings, silently suffering hunger pangs. Sometimes they would offer him a cup of tea. The children were average students. With a little effort they should be able to get through their exams.

Some days when he arrived there, he would find the house locked up. If he waited, assuming that they might have gone shopping and would be back shortly, there would be no sign of them even after half an hour. That they had gone off to a movie would be revealed to him only the next day. On occasions, if he went away after waiting for ten minutes, the next day they'd claim to have returned exactly on the fifteenth minute. On some days, when they had guests visiting or there was a good show on TV, they'd ask for the classes to be cancelled.

On occasions, the seth would ask him to stay back after classes. He'd then ask Shanmugam to write letters on his behalf or to prepare bills. He had a portable typewriter at home. Some days, when he took his leave, they'd hand him an aluminium vessel containing wheat and request him to hand it to a mill on his way home. He shouldn't forget to collect the ground wheat flour the next day on his way back to the tuition classes. The charges for grinding the wheat were one and a half rupees. If they didn't reimburse him on their own, he felt diffident about asking them for this amount.

It would be eight-thirty or nine by the time he returned home. This precluded him from participating in the daily cooking activities. Even though the others did not make a big deal out of this, he felt instinctively guilty. When he offered to do the dishes instead, they wouldn't let him.

Since the seth's brother was about Shanmugam's size, they put a pair of his used trousers and shirts in a bag and gave it to him. He felt reluctant to accept the items but, at the same time, lacked the will to refuse them. Even though their offer might have been out of pity at the sight of his own clothes, he somehow felt slighted.

When he unpacked them upon reaching home, he found the clothes were not as shabby as those he currently wore. Reassuring himself, he tried them on. They fitted him to a tee. He felt the trousers were slightly loose around the waist, but it was nothing a belt or a piece of rope couldn't fix.

The next day he wore his 'new' clothes to work. Did he notice a snide smile on Acharya's lips or was it merely his imagination? It seemed to him as though everyone in the office was continuously staring at him. Reuben came up and whispered, "Did the seth give you these?" He could only smile weakly in reply.

Since he might end up spending his tuition fee if he collected it every month, he had asked the seth to hang on to it till he decided to go home. When the April examinations were over, the seth paid him only four hundred rupees instead of the agreed upon four hundred and twenty. He wanted to question the discrepancy but couldn't.

Shanmugam applied for his accumulated twenty-one days' earned leave.

It was a Saturday. Half-a-day's work at the office. He took special permission to leave the office at twelve o' clock and reached home by twelve forty-five. Shenbagam hadn't gone on his rice run that day. Kamatchi had taken the day off. Muthu had also come home early with permission from his shop.

His trunk was already packed. Shenbagam had prepared the food for his journey. For the first night, it was rice with yogurt. For breakfast the next morning, there were chapatis with a dry curry for accompaniment. For lunch on the second day, there was tamarind rice. For dinner that night, he would purchase food packets at Chengalpattu. The next morning he would reach Tirunelveli and could have hot idlis at Central Café near the railway station.

Many passengers, whose destinations lay beyond Tirunelveli, would bathe in the Thamirabarani river to wash off the dust of the train journey, change and then proceed by bus. Several persons bound for places such as Nanguneri, Kalakkad, Panakudi, Valliyur, Ervadi, Vadakkankulam and so on have mentioned this to him. But Shanmugam had no intention of wasting half a day on this. If the train reached Tirunelveli by 8.00 or 8.30, and he caught the 9 o'clock bus, he would be in Nagercoil by 11.00. From there he could catch the 11.30 bus or put on the dog and arrive home grandly in a taxi. By 12.00 he would be home, time for a bath followed by lunch and a siesta thereafter.

Initially he thought he wouldn't write home and announce his arrival. He wanted to suddenly appear before them and watch his mother's face reflect a mixture of shock, surprise and happiness. But he had second thoughts on the subject. Throughout the two and half years, every letter from home contained the query 'when are you coming home?' In the circumstances he decided that the pleasure he derived from counting down the number of days should not be denied to his family members as well.

Money was a major problem. Of what use was the seth's four hundred rupees? Every which way he calculated, the total expenses still came to over a thousand rupees.

He had to borrow the needed cash, there was no alternative. If there was a law against travelling home on borrowed money, 90% of the migrant labourers here, the human flotsam, could never hope to get out of this place. Everyone borrowed money to get to their native places – whether it was a Tamilian going to Tirunelveli or Salem or a gurkha who'd travel up to Gorakhpur and then trek for over fifteen days carrying his luggage on his head to reach Nepal, the Marwari cook who'd get off at Sawai Madhopur and take another train to reach Jaipur, the milk-bhaiyas bound for Chandila or Barabanki in Uttar Pradesh or the Maharshtrian 'ghatis' travelling to Malvan or Chiplun.

The firm ran a Diwali fund. You paid ten rupees every month towards it. Every staff member had a share. Loans amounting to hundred, two hundred and even five hundred were disbursed out of the fund, depending upon the total amount in the pot and the borrower's contribution. The rate of interest was five percent. The first month's interest was deducted at the time of the loan itself. Shanmugam was not a participant. Reuben borrowed two hundred rupees and gave them to him.

Shenbagam returned his earlier loan. Kamatchi lent a hundred rupees. Next to the grocery shop where Muthu was employed was a Tamil tailor. Apart from tailoring he also stocked bolts of cloth. On the understanding that he would pay the cost of material and stitching charges in three instalments, Shanmugam had him run up two trousers and two half-sleeved shirts. He really preferred full-sleeved shirts, but the short sleeves saved a quarter metre of cloth.

He took Reuben to Grant Road and purchased two pairs of undervests, underwear and handkerchiefs, a pair of shoes for thirty-five rupees and two pairs of socks for ten rupees, a new lungi and a towel. The old trunk was still serviceable. An airbag for twenty rupees, shaving cream, brush, blades, toothbrush and toothpaste, a small bottle of hair cream, a small tin of Pond's talcum powder, train ticket – all these swallowed up two hundred rupees.

He would need money for casual expenses during the onward journey. He had to budget for the return train ticket and travel expenses. He took Kamatchi with him to Gandhi Market and bargained hard to purchase clothes for Appa, Amma, his brothers and sisters.

After everything was done, he had two hundred rupees left in his pocket. He needed to buy something for the house. Also, he couldn't go empty-handed when visiting relatives. He'd also need money for his personal expenses while at home. He wondered whether he could cope with all these outlays. What would he do if his appa or amma suddenly asked for fifty or a hundred rupees for some reason? Where would he then go for his return expenses?

He realised suddenly that when he set foot in Bombay again, he would be in hock for five hundred rupees. It would take him at least a year to pay the debts off.

When the train departed the station, his panic gave way to a strange new feeling of independence. As the Madras Express left Dadar Station exactly at 2.30, his pangs of separation suddenly hit him harder. Even though he had already taken leave of Shenbagam, Muthu and Kamatchi who had all come to see him off, he still looked out of the train's window, smiled and waved his hand.

The train, which moved slowly from Dadar till Matunga, picked up a sudden burst of speed once it crossed Sion. As he came and sat down in his seat, checked his possessions once again to make sure they were secure and stretched out his legs expansively, he felt a sense of relief, happiness and eagerness.

—

www.ingramcontent.com/pod-product-compliance
Lightning Source LLC
Chambersburg PA
CBHW030321160726
47992CB00005B/2105